LOVING THE MOUNTAIN MAN

ADRIANA ANDERS

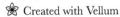

CONTENTS

To Le Husband:
Je t'aime.

CHRISTA

I'd thought my boss peeing off the deck at our annual Christmas party was the worst thing that would happen that day.

Boy, was I wrong.

Something had felt off the moment I'd arrived at Jonathan's massive cabin in the middle of nowhere. I was all nervous, gussied up for my first work event, hoping to make an impression. After a harrowing ten minutes spent navigating his steep, twisty drive, my wipers working double time to clear what I hoped was just a light rain, I'd pulled up and stared at the two the lone car parked in front of the house.

Where was everyone?

I spent the next three minutes listing all the reasons I shouldn't turn around and drive home, change out of this suffocating dress, put on my reindeer pajamas, and watch *Elf* for the millionth time. I'd make hot cocoa, stir it with a candy cane, and counter all that sugar with super salty popcorn.

I sighed. I'd spent hours shopping for the right dress and shoes for this shindig. Gran would kill me if I ran home with my tail between my legs.

Okay. So, fine, I'd come all the way out here. I'd go in, have one drink and a couple mini-quiches, and chat with my colleagues about... I shut my eyes tightly. Weather. Sports. Work. Hobbies.

I could do this.

I stepped out of the car into—*dear God—icy* cold, at least ten degrees cooler than down in the valley. Cursing myself for grabbing my dressy coat, instead of the warm one, I teetered up the pea gravel walkway to the massive wood and stone house, and rang the doorbell.

I'd just about given up when my boss, Jonathan, answered the door.

"Well, if it isn't the new girl." He stumbled, turned it into a dance, and reached for my coat. "Hey, New Girl. Let's get this off you."

"Oh. Oh, hi. Thank you." I shuffled back, avoiding his hands, and shoved the bottle of wine I'd brought at him. "This is for you. Where can I..."

"Bring it in, New Girl!" He grabbed the wine and coat and led the way into a big, open room, where he proceeded to serve me a bourbon (I asked for wine), and invited me to sit.

We were alone—him, me, and a massive,

reflective wall of windows at the opposite end of the sparsely modern space. And he was drunk.

I looked around, nervous. "So, where is everyone?"

"Yeah, not sure."

Time to get out of here.

I set down my drink and shuffled toward the door. "Look, I should go. This is—"

"Nah, nah. Come here, New Girl." He moved toward the windows. "Let me show you something."

By then, my fight-or-flight instincts were screaming at me to get out of there, while my keep-the-job-it-took-me-months-to-find instincts kept me frozen.

Should have listened to the first voice and run.

"You've gotta see this view."

"When are the others getting here, again?" I took a final, mad look around before he grabbed my arm and hauled me toward the French doors, which led out onto a huge deck. It was freezing.

"Party's cancelled. Didn't I tell you?" He threw out an arm and spun toward the big, black expanse beyond the circle of light pouring from inside. "Check out my incredible view while I..."

As soon as I recognized the sound of his fly unzipping, my awkward misgivings became outright fear.

Jonathan groaned. "Shit, man!" he said, as if I were his frat boy peanut gallery. "Too cold to piss out here."

Oh, good God. My boss was trying to pee all over his view. In front of me. *No freaking way.* I was out of there.

Back inside, I spent a frantic couple of minutes by the front door, searching for my coat. Crap, where did he put it? At least I had my purse, still over my shoulder. But I loved that coat.

"Hey, New Girl. Christa, Christa, Christa… hang on, come on back, hun." He was suddenly there, in my space, hands on my shoulders, as if he had a right to touch me. "Let's figure out—" I yanked my arm from his hold and his expression morphed from good-natured to something sly. I stepped away. A shiver went through me as I followed the direction of his gaze. "Oh, look. *Mistletoe.*"

That's when he put his hand on my boob and tried to kiss me.

I'd always asked myself how I'd react if someone attacked me. Well, now I knew.

I lost it. My chest rose and fell on wordless grunts, as my hands flailed, slapping his face and chest. I shoved him into the corner, kicked him hard between the legs, threw open the front door, and took off down the walk, over the stupid little rocks—it was a wonder I didn't break an ankle, or a heel—and into my car. The Jetta started on the first try, a total miracle given how freaking *cold* it was out here. Shuddering like crazy, I barreled down the precarious drive, fast.

Don't follow me, I begged the whole time, eyes flicking to the rearview. *Please don't chase me.*

It wasn't until I left the gravel and hit the pavement of the main road that my car swerved. It took about ten seconds for the words *black ice* to enter my brain but by then, I'd lost control. Everything spun, dark shapes sped by, something squealed.

My tires? No. No, the sound was coming from me.

I pushed my foot hard to the brake pedal and in a flash remembered some lesson from a driving class about pumping, not stomping. I did it, somehow; tapped that pedal over and over again, worked it like a jackhammer.

In eerie slow-motion, I skidded for what felt like ages, straight toward the cliff's edge, pivoted left and…

Stopped.

Oh, thank God.

My hands wouldn't come off the steering wheel, as if, no matter how hard my brain told them it was safe, they couldn't quite believe it.

"That's okay. It's okay." I said the words aloud, trying to calm myself, I guess. To still my jittery hands.

But man, this was a *lot* for one night.

The shivering took over, clacking my teeth together as fast and wooden as Pinocchio on speed. Okay, that was a weird analogy, even for me.

I should probably calm down, wait here for a few seconds, catch my breath, regroup, maybe call Gran to explain what had happened, that I was scared, that this whole night was a clust—

The car shifted, tilted, screeched so loud I flattened my hands to my ears.

Sudden quiet. Stillness.

Oh, God, my chest. Why can't I breathe?

Something was very wrong.

I blinked, opened my eyes, focused on my hands. I'd moved them again, apparently. One gripped the gear shift, the other had a tight hold on the door handle.

Okay. Okay. *Focus.*

Oh…shit.

Slowly, like a spotlight illuminating a dark set, engulfing one new detail at a time, my brain took in the situation.

I was hanging, my body listing to the right, held in place by the seatbelt. I'd wedged my legs into the space under the wheel. The entire world tilted at a crazy angle. The high-beams tunneled through air. Nothing but air.

Slowly, barely shifting at all, I looked left, first with my eyeballs, then craning my neck. Was I imagining that light or was it real? Was someone coming? *Let it be someone coming.*

When it disappeared, despair melted through me, turning my limbs to lead. Not a light. The night sky, glowing pink, like just before a snow.

I whimpered, shoved down my desire to thrash like a bug in a web, and swallowed hard.

Okay. Okay, this wasn't so bad. I could call someone. I unpeeled my right hand from the stick, reached out, patted the console, gingerly.

No phone. Further to the right, over the passenger seat, I let my fingers travel, more and more certain that I was screwed until...

Oh, holy mother of God, yes. I was in a high-stakes game of Operation—only instead of avoiding the edges, the object was not to rock the car—I slid my hand into my purse, grasped my phone and, slowly pulled it close enough to peer at the screen.

No service.

Please, no. Oh, please please please, God.

Eyes squeezed shut, I swallowed back a fresh bout of hysteria. *Don't shake, don't move a muscle. Think, dammit!*

Okay. I opened my eyes again, blinked.

No bars right here, but if I could get out of the car and walk—never mind these *stupid* shoes —I could find shelter. Or one measly little bar. Enough to get a text out. Or an emergency call. Something.

Sucking in a big, shaky breath, I reached for the handle, pulled, and pushed. Wouldn't budge.

Oh, hell.

Fueled by desperation, I hit the unlock button, jolted at the sound, and tried again.

Nothing.

I can't die. There's too much I haven't done. Too many promises I've made myself.

And what about Gran? She couldn't handle another shock. *Oh, God, please someone, help.*

Eyes wide now, the inevitability of it turning everything crystal clear, I stared up. Granny Evans would spend Christmas alone, worrying about me.

Something shifted above and I shut my eyes only to be assaulted by images of my body, smashed and ruined, at the bottom of this ravine. Wherever the hell this place was. I couldn't even picture it on a map. And for some reason, not knowing where I was about to die made it all worse.

A scuffing noise, gritty like dirt on a road, made me open my eyes.

Was that a person up there?

2

MICAH

I eyed the car, wedged between a four-foot rock ledge and a young lodgepole pine. Christ, the asshole was lucky.

It was tempting to let him fend for himself, considering where he'd built his stupid McCabin. Damned thing was an eyesore.

I took a few steps closer, over ice-slicked asphalt, before looking over the side. Shit. Didn't look stable. I'd need to climb down.

Yanking off my gloves, I eyed the night-dark rock face. I could get down this, no problem. Getting another person up, however…

No point worrying right now.

I let my legs drop over the side, hands gripping the edge, found a quick foothold, and shifted my weight. Another shift, another foothold, one hand, then the other. Piece of cake.

We'd see how it'd be with whoever was in that car.

Couldn't be the new neighbor. Rich dudes didn't drive Volkswagens. Probably line 4 in their stupid handbook, with an asterisk pointing to allowed vehicles: Audis and Suburbans and Kawasaki motorcycles. Fucking Jeeps.

Something moved below, with a sound of grinding metal. Damn thing was about to go.

I picked up my pace. My foot hit the first tuft of grass and I dropped, then quickly walked the last few feet to the car.

"You okay in there?" I called out, my voice over-loud in the ice-shrouded quiet.

A woman's voice sounded from inside, the words unclear.

"Get the door open?" I squinted through the fogged-up glass to see her shake her head. Shit.

"Window?"

Another shake.

I stepped back, looking at the big picture. It wasn't just the ledge and tree—a chain-link fence held the car in place. Good.

"You got a coat or something?"

The woman didn't react at first.

"Got a scarf or a blanket? Put it over your head." I reached for my Leatherman. "Gonna break the window."

I watched as she pulled something from around her neck and covered her body.

"Ready?"

I gave her a couple seconds and tapped the

glass, hard. In an instant, it cracked, blurring the space between us even more.

"Push it out with the scarf."

Once she'd shoved the glass outside, I reached in and tried the door. No luck. "Sure it's unlocked?"

"Yeah." The woman's voice was breathless, almost a whisper.

"Can you unbuckle?"

"Kinda...hanging from the belt." She sounded breathless. Scared as hell.

"Can you hold yourself up? Use the other seat if you have to." I put out a hand and paused. "Okay if I hold your arm?"

A pause and then another nod.

It took her a few seconds, which was understandable. Finally, holding up her weight so she wouldn't fall against the passenger door and knock the whole damned car down, she unbuckled.

"You get your arms around me?"

"But..." Her voice was high and strained, like she could barely get the words out. "I'm...holding myself up."

"Use your legs to stay steady."

"Right. Okay." Her eyes met mine. They were huge; so deep they looked black. "I can't fit through the window."

"You'll fit." That was one of the funny things about survival. Didn't matter what size she was.

She'd fit through a damn porthole if she wanted it bad enough. "Grab me on three."

With a grimace, she shifted her weight, steadied herself, and put a hand out.

The car moved. Felt like a fucking earthquake. Or a missile strike.

I didn't think. No time. Just grasped her under the arms and pulled. Not fast enough. She caught on something.

"Push off! Use your legs." I yelled, picturing the carnage if I couldn't get her out. "*Push!*"

Everything happened at once—the car sliding, the woman tightening her hold on my waist, while one hand grasped mine. Then, slow as a tree falling, the car slid, slowly at first, then picking up speed as it smashed a pinball path to the bottom of the ravine. I threw us back against the dry, grassy bank, where we landed in a rough heap.

We lay still long after the last echo from below.

I caught my breath enough to ask, "You okay?"

"Think so." Her voice was barely a whisper.

"In one piece?" She shook a little and I tightened my hold. Shit. She didn't have a coat on. "Can you move?"

She nodded against my chest.

"Come on."

The trip back up was tougher—as I'd known it would be. A dozen steps through dry, tufted grass, to the bottom of the rock face.

"You climb?"

She shook her head. *Shit.*

"Okay. You go first. Put a foot here."

She moved to do it, then stopped, swayed for a couple seconds, and grabbed my hand. I gripped it hard. "Lost a shoe."

Not only had she lost one, but the other was a high heel—pointy and red and totally useless out here. Useless anywhere.

"Kick it off."

She did it quickly, then turned to the rock. She'd never make it in that dress—a short, tight, sparkly number. I was about to say something when she yanked it up over her hips, giving me an unexpected glimpse of her rear.

I turned away.

"I can do this," she said more to herself than to me.

After a couple false starts, she got a few feet up and stopped.

"Stuck."

"Next foothold's there." I glanced up, forcing my eyes to focus past her body to the rock itself. "About three feet up."

She bent her leg, pushed up on it, and reached, but it was too far.

"I'll help you. Just be ready to shove up with your legs and grip."

"Okay."

I put one hand on her butt, the other hovered behind her back—just in case—and pushed. "Go."

For a millisecond, she teetered and looked like she'd fall straight back, but finally her balance changed, she hugged the wall, and she was up. Almost. Another half a minute and she was over the edge. I followed her to the top and found her sitting huddled in on herself.

"Let's go."

"Oh. Right." She blinked down to where her car was gone—where she'd almost bit it herself—and let out a choked little laugh. Even in the dark, I could see the shell-shocked expression of someone whose mind hadn't caught up with events. "I might need a rest first."

"Yeah. Just not here."

I leaned down and offered my hand. "Let's go before you freeze your"—I cleared my throat —"butt off."

It wasn't until she struggled to standing and pulled her minuscule dress down around her hips that I remembered her lack of shoes.

Hell.

I bent, grabbed her wrist with my right hand and put the left through her legs, before hauling her over my shoulders.

3

CHRISTA

*W*as this man saving me? Or had my life just gone from hellish to worse?

"Um, sir? I can walk." My voice came out reedy and weak. "Would you mind putting me down…please?"

"Soon as we get to my place."

"Your place?" All the blood was going to my head, making my words slow. My tongue felt thick. I should have been frantic, but I couldn't seem to get a scream going. "I need to call the cops."

"No cell service here. Call 'em from my home phone."

"Please. I'll walk."

He set me on the ground and steadied me before taking his hands away. "You got no shoes."

I looked down. Oh. *Right.* No wonder it was so cold. That and my lost coat.

"Won't hurt you. Promise. You want to walk, you walk." I blinked at him. He was dressed appropriately for the frigid night in a dark canvas coat with a thick beanie pulled low. His face, covered in a dense beard, didn't need much else. His bottom half, in jeans and mud-stained boots, looked just as warm. "Here." He unzipped his coat and, before I could stop him, put it over my quaking shoulders. Oh my God, it was Heaven. "Sorry I didn't ask."

I waited. "Ask what?"

"Permission to pick you up. Usually…" He paused and shook his head. "Never mind."

What kind of person had a *usually* that involved heaving bodies over their enormous slab of a shoulder? A fireman? A serial kidnapper? "You carry…people…a lot?" The words didn't want to slide out past my chattering teeth.

"Used to." He shrugged, then glanced at my feet. "Boots are big, but you can—"

Before he could take off his shoes for me, I stopped him with a hand on his shoulder. "No. No, I'll walk like this."

"You could just let me carry you." He looked up the mountain, to wherever our destination was. "Be faster."

"I'm heavy. I don't want you to—"

"Light as a feather."

I was shuddering too hard to give him a look.

"Come on."

"Not killing your…back? You swear?"

"Swear."

"Not planning any…nefarious activities?" I tried to make it into a joke, but my voice came out tiny and scared.

"Don't even know what that means."

"You're not going to—"

"Kidding." His mouth did a weird quirking thing at the corners, which I assumed was meant to be a smile. It didn't look entirely natural on him. "Won't hurt you. Promise on the memory of everyone I've ever lost." Every word sounded dead serious.

Which I guess it would if he were a creepy person, bent on killing me, but considering that I couldn't feel my toes—or my brain—anymore, it was definitely one of those leap of faith moments. Just those words—leap of faith—sent my mind careening back to the moment he pulled me from the car.

I nodded. He grabbed my hand and bent, and suddenly I was on his back again, my butt by his head.

He huffed on—actually up—each uneven step jolting me against him, and I could do nothing but curl into his heat.

"Not far," he huffed out. A few minutes later, I smelled wood smoke just as a dog barked, the sound muffled. I strained my neck to look ahead.

It was a log cabin, its windows glowing warmly. There was someone waiting there for him, surely. A woman, all snug in that home, dinner simmering on the stove. Or, not dinner, maybe, since it was late, but a hot chocolate or something.

I'd sell my soul for a hot chocolate right now. Anything hot.

I almost laughed. It would be really weird if I laughed right now, wouldn't it?

At the cabin door, he let me down slowly. Boneless, I collapsed immediately against him.

"Can't…feel…feet." My teeth clacked together with each word.

He threw open the door to a madly barking dog, who looked—I squinted—*happy*. Something clawed at my knee and I looked down. Oh. Two dogs. A big German Shepherd-type creature and, beside it…was that one of those papillons? I blinked. A one-eared papillon.

"Back it up, girls."

Slowly, I turned to look up at him. "Me?"

"Talking to the dogs." He turned to them. "Brownie, quit it!"

The big dog stopped jumping on him, moved back a few feet, and sat.

"Bear, down."

Once Bear—the little one—complied, going to sit next to her companion, he and I went in. He shut the door, enclosing us in quiet—aside from the crackling of a wood stove—and blessed warmth.

"Might wanna…" He lowered his chin toward my feet. "Get that thing off."

Thing? I glanced down, puzzled, until I realized what he meant. My tights, full of runs, with big holes in them now, choked my toes. I couldn't feel them.

"Have a seat. I'll heat up water for a tea." He paused. "Get you something to put on."

I nodded, swayed, put a hand out, and caught myself on the door. Oh. Boneless.

"I can't…" I peered at the sofa. I mean, the place was tiny, so it wasn't far, but it looked miles away. I tried a step, but it sent shooting pain up my foot and I was much, much too tired. Or something more than that—beyond pain and exhaustion, into some kind of otherness.

I sank to my butt, right there, against the door.

My savior walked back into the room with a few folded-up items, and stopped when he saw me. "Bath?"

I shook my head. "Pro'ly drown."

"Okay. Well, um. Here." Slowly, he drew close, like he might approach a wild animal. He set a pile of neatly-folded fabric beside me, picked up one item—a soft plaid blanket—and put it over me, then handed me the telephone he'd stuck in his back pocket. "Call whoever you need to."

I stared at the phone, suddenly unsure of who I should reach out to. Granny Evans, definitely, since she'd start worrying eventually.

"What time is it?" I asked.

"'Bout nine thirty."

I blinked. "You're kidding." What time had I left the party? Eight, I'd thought. Maybe eight thirty?

Something else occurred to me. "How'd you find me?"

"Opened the door to let the dogs out. Heard you skid off the road. Took me a while to find you."

Something broke loose inside my chest and I couldn't keep my head up. With an audible thunk, my forehead hit my knees. I was shaking, only not from the cold this time.

Was I crying? I turned my head, wiped my face and stared at my palm. Definitely wet.

How did I not know what my body was doing?

"Hey, hey. Don't do that."

I couldn't stop because I couldn't even tell it was happening. How was that for messed up?

He crouched in front of me, framed by his dogs, and I noticed his feet. He wore slippers. Grey, flannel slippers, the most out of place thing I could imagine on this big brute of a man.

"What…Uh… Hell. Please don't do that. What can I do?" he asked, sounding totally out of his element.

After everything that had happened tonight— my shithead boss trying to put his hands on me, then, oh, just driving off the side of a mountain, nearly *dying*, and being hauled back to life by this guardian angel person—I couldn't drum up the tiniest drop of fear or suspicion.

All I wanted was a hug.

"Could you," I managed through chattering teeth. "Please hold me?"

4

MICAH

*S*he wanted me to wrap my arms around her. As if I did shit like that every day.

No. No fucking way. I was good with pulling people out of wreckage and just fine humping them up the mountain to safety, but aftercare wasn't something I had experience with.

"Uh…look. Why don't we ca—"

Before I could finish, she'd moved from her spot against the front door to my lap, leaving me with no choice but to wrap myself around her shaking body.

So, she wasn't having the brush off. Brownie and Bear moved closer to sniff our unexpected visitor. Wasn't surprising, since this was the only female we'd ever had here.

The woman had to be in shock. Not much to do about that, except make sure she was physically safe. Warm, hydrated.

After nudging the girls away, I grabbed the

blanket from the floor and put it over her—us—trying not to catch that warm, addictive smell I hadn't gotten a hit of in forever. Damn, it was good. A drug to a man who'd been sober for years. I had the sudden urge to lick her.

Which just proved how unfit for this I was.

She rubbed her face tighter to my chest and pressed hard against me.

At least she wasn't scared of me anymore. Though, she really should've called the cops before trusting me like this.

"Hold on." I leaned over and grabbed my phone from where she'd dropped it. "Hey, um…" Jesus, what was her name? I didn't even know that. Didn't know a damned thing about her. "Call the cops. Let 'em know what happened."

She nodded, but didn't move to take the phone. I should do it.

Just a sec.

Another of those close snuggles brought her ass tight to my crotch and I stilled. Yeah, no. This wasn't going to work. They needed to come get her.

"Look, I'll give 'em a call." I dialed 911 and spoke as soon as the operator answered.

"Not an emergency, ma'am. Just wanted to report an accident—no injuries."

"Go ahead, sir."

Shit, I'd forgotten to get her name. I leaned in. "What's your name?"

She mumbled something against my chest.

"Crystal?"

"Christa. Evans."

"Woman named Christa Evans. Wiped out on Pine Mountain Road. Her car..." Shit. Her car was at the bottom of the fucking ravine. I couldn't help tightening my arm around her, then cleared my throat to get rid of some leftover adrenaline. "Black ice on the mountain. Her vehicle's gone."

"Can you put Ms. Evans on the phone, sir?"

"Just a sec." I pulled the blanket away and handed her the phone, instantly missing the distance between us. "Go on and tell them."

"Hello?" She glanced up at me for a few seconds, then away. "Yeah. Christa Evans." She rattled off an address and appeared to listen. "He's..." Her eyes met mine. They were dark in her pale face, bottomless. "Are you Mr. Micah Graham?"

I nodded.

"Yes." Another long pause. "He saved me. Risked his life. I'll be fine... Yes. Oh. Okay. Thanks for letting me know. Thank you."

She handed me the phone and I listened, while the operator informed me they'd try to get someone up here, but since it wasn't an emergency, it likely wouldn't be tonight. I was also advised not to drive, given the driving conditions.

All the while, the woman—Christa—watched me. She had one of those round faces turned into a heart by a pointy little chin. All of it was sort of framed by super-straight, shoulder-length hair, cut across her forehead. Reminded me of that actress in Pulp Fiction. Except fuller, her rosy cheeks and bright, almost-black eyes making her doll-like. The rest of her was nothing like a doll. Or if it was, it wasn't one I'd give my kid sister.

"They don't want us driving tonight. Said the roads are mess in the valley, too."

"Oh, crap." Something like panic flitted across her face. "I don't want to put you out, it's not—"

"It's fine."

"I'm sorry, Micah."

"Don't be." I nodded. "Christa."

"I'm safe with you, right?"

"Always."

A big, fat tear formed at the outside corner of her eye and rolled down her cheek. I don't think she even noticed it. "Thank you, Micah."

"Any time."

With a deep, shaky sigh, she got close again. It took a few seconds for me to realize she wasn't using me for heat and comfort this time, she was thanking me.

After what had to be close to a minute, I shifted back. "You, uh, ready for some tea?"

She sniffed and nodded, let me nudge her off me and get up. I offered her a hand, which she accepted, and pulled her to standing.

"Mind if I call my roommate, Micah?"

"Course. I'll get you something hot." I handed her the phone.

With the girls dogging my footsteps—as usual —I went into the kitchen. Well, what I thought of as my kitchen, but she'd probably see as something less. Sink, oven, counter—all shoved into the corner of the cabin's main room. At least I'd made the bathroom separate. And the bedroom. Which would give her some privacy.

'Cause she wasn't going anywhere tonight.

5

CHRISTA

I dialed home, hating that I'd be interrupting Gran's shows.

She picked up on the second ring, a little out of breath. "Hello?"

"Hey, Gran."

"Christa, hon? What are you doing?"

I sighed and walked to the front window. Crap, the sky was that same weird pink. I glanced back at Micah—my guardian angel—and let the curtain fall closed before shutting my eyes and concentrating on *not* giving my grandmother another heart attack.

"First of all, I want you to know that I'm safe. I'm fine. Okay?"

"What the hell's going on?"

"Got into an accident, leaving the work party." She tried to talk and I pushed through. "I'm totally fine. Unhurt." Not strictly true, but she didn't need to know about my sore wrist and the shoulder I could barely move, or about the pain across my chest from where the seatbelt had held me back. It suddenly occurred to me, in a weird aside, that my airbag hadn't deployed. Probably a good thing, given the situation. Last thing I'd need on top of this was a broken nose. "But the car's…gone."

Silence.

"Gran?"

"Gone," she repeated, without inflection. So much for not freaking her out. No way would I tell her about the stuff that happened before I left my boss's house. *Ex-boss*.

"There's black ice up here. Hairpin curves. I braked and…" I shut my eyes hard against the wave of nausea that overtook me, took a step back and made it to the sofa, where I collapsed with an *oof*. My voice came out flat. "Went off the side of a cliff, Gran." I paused, expecting some kind of reaction. Nothing. I'd killed her. "You still there?"

"Yes. Go on. How are you calling me?"

"A man saved me. Gran, he's my…" Angel, I almost said, but some instinct told me he wouldn't like that. "Micah." His eyes were on me. I could feel it, though I couldn't look at him right now or I'd lose it. "He…" *Don't cry. Keep it in.* "He climbed down a sheer rock face. Um, broke the car window, and, uh, pulled me out." *Hiccup.* "Just as it dropped." I inhaled, wishing I'd learned how to meditate, or actually gone to all those yoga classes I'd signed up for. "The car. The car dropped."

"He there?" She used her all business voice.

"Yeah."

"Put him on."

"No, he's…"

"Put. Him. On. Christa. I need to talk to the man who saved my baby's life."

"Um. Micah?" I held the phone out. "My Grandmother would like to talk to you."

Expressionless, he stepped to the sofa, took the phone and said, "This is Micah Graham."

He didn't say much. A couple *Yes, ma'ams* and *No, ma'ams*. The man had a good voice. Solid, but not overloud. Deep, and smooth… No, that wasn't the right word. More like *rich*. Like a strong cup of black coffee. No freaking watered down lattes for this man.

I blinked. Was I delirious, comparing this man's voice to a hot drink? These seemed an awful lot like the thoughts of a person teetering on the edge.

Oh, God, don't think of edges right now.

One of the dogs—the big one. Brownie, I think?—nudged at my knee. I petted her unconsciously and sank deep into the sofa. It was one of those big, man-sized pieces of furniture. Soft and ridiculously comfortable. I tucked my legs under me and scratched behind the dog's ear. It was soft, the movement repetitive and soothing.

Micah spoke quietly into the phone. I could fall asleep to this.

"Here," he said. My eyes popped open just as he put the phone into my hand.

"Oh. Thanks."

"You there?" Gran sounded solid as a rock. Nothing could shock the woman. I wanted to be her when I grew up.

"Yeah."

"You trust that man?"

I kept my gaze on the dog, remembering the feel of Micah's hand holding mine, pulling me out of that death trap.

"Yes. I do."

She exhaled on a long, low whistle. "There's black ice all over the place. Non-stop sirens in town. You're stuck there tonight, honey." I opened my mouth to respond, but she barreled on. "He appears to be a decent young man, but I'm going to make some calls. He gave a reference —guy down at the Veteran's Center. Kurt Anderson. Says he'll vouch for him. I'll call, just to make sure. I'll also talk to the police in case he has a record or anything. And maybe they can get someone up there tonight, but…" She finally paused and I could picture her expression. The tight-lipped look that said she was holding everything inside. Her next words came out fast and rougher than I'd ever heard her. "I can't lose you, Christa. Not after your dad. I can't lose you, honey. Just stay put. Don't try to go anywhere in this weather."

"It's Christmas Eve tomorrow, Gran."

"I know. I know, sweetie. You stay safe. Gus is here. It'll be the two of us and that's fine." Since he'd moved into the neighborhood a few months before, Gus spent most waking hours with her anyway, so it wouldn't be a stretch. "I'd rather know you're safe and alive than worry about you flying off the side of a cliff again. Stay with that young man. Okay?"

"Yes." I looked at Micah, who was busy doing something in his kitchen.

"He tries anything, you remind him of the promise he made. Got it?"

"What promise?"

"Yep. All right. Better get cracking. Love you. Bye, sweetie." Typical Gran, ignoring what she didn't want to hear. She hung up, leaving me staring at the phone in one hand and scratching the dog with the other.

"Here." Micah set a cup on an end table, took the phone from me and set it within my reach. "You hungry?"

I shook my head but then my belly rumbled and I gave him a sheepish smile. "I don't want to put you out." As if I hadn't put him out already.

"It's fine." He went to the kitchen and returned with a steaming bowl, which he handed to me. After putting a couple logs into the wood stove, he went and grabbed his own bowl, finally settling at a small wooden table to eat.

It would be polite to go and join him instead of staying here. But it was warm in front of the fire, with this plaid blanket thrown over my legs, the small one-eared dog on top off it, the big one pressing her head to my knee. Unbelievably cozy.

I wasn't sure I could move.

6

MICAH

*W*ould she like the stew? Was venison something she enjoyed or was she one of those city people who couldn't stand the taste of game? And she *was* a city person. That was for sure. That slick haircut, with its sharp edges, the short, sparkly dress. That single shoe she'd had on before shucking it. The spike heel.

City girl.

I scraped the bottom of my bowl, trying to figure out what someone with fancier taste buds would think. Salty, thick, rich, meaty. I liked it. The dogs liked it. Good enough.

She was stuck with me now anyway, so she'd have to be okay with it.

Her eyes went to mine before looking back at her stew, reminding me of a little animal; a little scared, shy, skittish.

"How you feeling?"

She appeared to consider. "Amazingly well. Thanks."

"Yeah? No aches? Anything hurt?"

She turned her head and stopped short with a grimace. "Everything?"

I went to the bathroom and the kitchen, then came back with a supersize bottle of ibuprofen and a glass of water. "Take these." I handed her four. I'd been in a couple accidents and I knew how bad that kind of shit hurt.

"That many?"

"You can do 800 for a couple days. Won't kill you." I knew this from experience.

She nodded, grabbed the pills, and was about to pop them into her mouth when I put a hand to hers to stop her. "Check 'em first."

"Huh?"

"The pills. Make sure they're what they're supposed to be."

It took her a second to get it, but when she did, her soft mouth hardened and she popped them without looking. "I trust you."

I lifted my brows.

She reached for the water, which she slugged down before glaring at me. "You'd have to chase after me with a chainsaw, wearing a hockey mask at this point to get me to stop trusting you."

The image startled me into a laugh. She had no idea how apt that image was. Chainsaws were pretty much my stock in trade.

I filled the empty glass and brought it back to her.

"Don't have to wait on me."

Not bothering to respond, I went and grabbed the pile of clothes I'd set beside her at the door. I didn't typically get embarrassed about my stuff, but the fabric on these was worn, washed, and faded like everything I owned. I'd picked the thermals because they were the tightest items I could think of, but suddenly I thought I might need to go back and see if I had anything more appropriate for a woman who wore glitter and had hair that looked like a wig.

I muttered something about a soak, went to the bathroom to turn the water on, and left the clothes in a pile on the radiator, along with a towel.

I took a second in the bathroom to regroup. I'd be fine with someone in my space. Just for a day or whatever. She seemed nice enough.

I stared myself down in the mirror. Bearded, gruff, and mean-looking. Jesus, what must she think?

Probably something close to the truth. That I was an uncivilized dude coping alone in the wilds of Washington State. Just surviving day to day.

She, however, was gorgeous. And, yeah, attractive women scared the hell out of me. But Jesus, no matter how much I wanted to grab the dogs and take off, leaving her the cabin, that wasn't an option. She needed help.

"Bath's ready," I said and grabbed her empty bowl from the side table. "No bubbles or any other fancy shit."

"Oh, look. I don't need a bath. I could just—"

"Trust me. You need it." The look she threw me said I was being pushy, so I explained. "It'll help your soreness. Left some clothes in there for you."

"Okay. Thank you." She reached out a hand and I stepped back, not daring to look at the questions I'd see on her face. "Look. Um, Micah. I'm sorry to barge in on you like this."

"Can't be helped."

"Well, I appreciate it."

I was probably supposed to fill the pause she left, but I couldn't come up with a single thing to say.

"As soon as the ice is gone, I'll call someone to get me, okay?"

I went into the bathroom before she could say anything else and shut off the tap. When I turned to leave, she stood in the doorway, blocking my exit. I cleared my throat to fill the silence.

"You have Christmas plans?"

I searched that earnest little heart face to see if she was kidding. "No." I couldn't remember the last time I'd celebrated Christmas. Or, actually, yeah. I could. Kabul, six years ago. Brown turkey in gelatinous gravy, spongy cornbread, mashed potatoes that were whiter than the tray and tasted like chalk. I'd had no idea I'd been spending my last Christmas as a soldier.

"Okay." A big inhale lifted her chest. Was she disappointed? "Well, then…okay."

She went into the bathroom and I shut the door, then stood there for a few seconds, trying to figure out what to do about the sleeping arrangements.

7

CHRISTA

h, God. I groaned and sank into the deep, hot water. Maybe I had died, after all, and this was heaven.

I'd eyed the tub before getting in because, though the cabin appeared neat, I'd had enough filthy ex-boyfriends that I didn't automatically trust a person's cleanliness. This one, apparently, was the exception to the rule. The tub was spotless. His soap selection left something to be desired, but I'd deal.

He'd saved my life. The man had a pass on everything. Forever.

And this felt amazing.

For a second, with my eyes closed, I let my mind wander, which was a mistake. A sound smacked me, loud as a freight train: screeching tires, smashing metal, breaking glass. I gasped and worked hard to catch my breath.

Freezing. Hurting. Loud. So loud. I threw my

hands up over my face, splashing water everywhere.

"You okay in there?"

Yes, I tried to say, but I was shaking too hard to use my voice. How could I possibly be cold in this hot, hot bath?

No. No, I'm not. I'm really not.

"Um. Christa. Hey." He knocked, the sound weirdly muted against the cacophony in my head. "Say something, okay?"

I turned, sloshing water out of the bath, and grasped the edge with both hands.

"I'm… Shit. I'm coming in." After a few seconds, the door flew open and he was there— really freaking tall, his shoulders wider than the doorway. His hair—the color of wet bark—was shorn about half an inch from his scalp, like he didn't have time to deal. He looked dark and angry and wild and, for one weird second, part of me left my tight-knuckled hold on the bath behind and let my body remember how his had felt beneath me.

I must've looked like hell because he didn't pause when he saw me, just swooped down and removed me from the bath like some towering God. Hercules or Poseidon or whatever. Water went everywhere, soaked him, the floor, but he didn't give a crap. From where he'd grabbed me under the armpits, he shifted, lifted, pulled me to him, and breathed.

Oh. Oh, I'm crying.

I'd never felt so out of control.

He tightened his hold and put an arm under my bottom to steady me, held me as easily as he would an infant, while I clawed at him and sobbed into his neck.

Big, loud, messy convulsions I hadn't experienced since I was a kid, before my dad died. Back when sobbing had served a purpose— getting emotion out into the air, cleansing it, maybe. After his death, there'd been no point in crying. Why bother, when no one heard me? When my insides were too shriveled to feel anything anyway?

His chest rumbled against mine and I tried, hard, to stop. To listen to whatever he was saying. But I couldn't. This wasn't a breakdown that I could stem using willpower. This was one of those all-encompassing things that hurt. Like really, really hurt. Had I broken a rib in the accident?

"Come on, honey. Come on." He was swaying, back and forth, shushing me in a quiet voice, trying his damnedest to soothe me. Who was this man who looked like he'd as soon tear a person apart as talk to them, and then rocked me like a baby? Like I was something precious.

Against my nose, the underside of his jaw was rough, as if he'd shaved there recently. It didn't smell like soap, though, but like… I sucked in a long, stuffy-nosed breath. He smelled like… The woods, maybe? Sawdust? And, God, that other thing. A man smell. His body. Earthy, but good.

Not sweat so much as...what was it? Pheromones, or something.

Holy shit, what am I doing?

I felt like a puppet, controlled by my own out-of-control emotions.

I let out another shuddering breath, shaking hard, and in that moment, became utterly aware that I was naked. In his arms. My nipples were almost painfully hard against the rough wool scrape of his flannel shirt.

Another scrape. Oh. Oh, God. Was I moaning? How was this happening? I tilted my head, despite myself, and let my top lip stroke that place that smelled so good. An urge took me over —*lick him*, it screamed, and I was about to, when his voice cut through what I could only think of as a fugue state.

"You okay?"

"I don't know," I said, truthfully. I was breathless, and still clogged with unshed tears.

"Come on." He turned to the side and took me to the right, into his bedroom, where he somehow managed to pull back the blanket while holding me. Slowly, and so carefully that I almost had to cry again, he put me in his bed, covered me, and left me alone in the dark.

I opened my mouth to ask him to stay and then reason finally kicked in and I shut it without uttering a word.

8

MICAH

*M*y instincts had played a big part in saving my life more than once. So I listened to them, usually. But tonight, I had to ignore the one begging me to go back and slide into bed next to that soft, naked body. To take her in my arms and hold her all night. Tightly, but carefully.

I paced to the door and back. There and back. On the third trip, I noticed the girls following me with their eyes, wide as I neared the front door, disappointed on my way back.

I let them out and sniffed. Smelled like snow.

I went and grabbed my phone—hated the goddamned thing, but I couldn't run my business without it—and checked the weather app.

Two feet. If they predicted that much down in the valley, then up here, we were in for a major blizzard. Best case scenario, I'd get her down the mountain in the morning, then make it back up before it hit.

I thought of what her grandmother had said to me on the phone. "You'll take care of my baby for me, won't you, Micah? You'll keep her safe?"

My "Yes, ma'am" had been automatic. Of course I'd keep her safe. It was what I did, keeping civilians safe.

Except not anymore. Unless I counted climbing trees to cut off dangerous branches as being for the good of the public. Which it wasn't. It was what I did for a living. To make money. To survive.

I sank to the sofa, face in hands, and waited for all the post-battle feelings to pass. My muscles were weak with it, loose the way they'd be after a drink. Which wasn't a bad idea.

I shoved back up to standing, went to the kitchen and pulled a beer out of the fridge. Then, after a couple seconds, I put it away and took out the hard stuff. Bourbon. It finally felt like the right time to open it.

Funny. Distracting me from a naked woman in my bed wasn't what I'd expected to use the bottle for. Maybe not so much a distraction as a private celebration. Or a thank you. To who or whatever had made me open the door right then. It was Bear, wasn't it? She'd barked, I'd opened the door, and then I'd heard the sound of crashing metal.

I set down the bottle and got out a couple

pieces of rawhide for my girls before pouring myself a massive drink. Then I turned off the lights, let girls back in, handed them each their treat, grabbed a couple blankets from the closet, and limped back to the sofa.

I took a few deep sips, set the glass aside, toed off my slippers, and stood up again to shuck my jeans. Then, with a sigh, I removed my prosthetic left leg, a process which took a few minutes.

It was weird, sitting here with my residual limb out, and the woman on the other side of the door. She could walk into the living room any second and see me.

I forced myself to stay like that—drinking the bourbon with bare legs, daring her, in some fucked up part of my brain to come out here. Would she have let me hold her, if she knew? Would she have cried in my arms? Would she still think of me as a hero?

Jesus. Idiot.

I slugged back the rest of the drink, enjoying the smell and smoky burn, and sprawled out under the blankets on the sofa, my eyes drawn to the flickering flames behind the wood stove's cloudy glass door.

Jesus, that had been close. Her face, when I'd first seen it…

I shut my eyes, but that was worse, because I could hear her. Those choked little whimpering sounds.

The freezing little hand in mine, as weak and fragile as a bird fallen from the nest.

My eyes flew open. I'd left my gloves down there, on the side of the road.

Whatever. Had another pair someplace.

And, fuck, what did a pair of gloves matter compared to what she'd gone through? She'd lost her damn vehicle.

I had a sudden urge to go check and make sure she hadn't lost anything else when her car had tried to suck her down the mountain. Anything else—like a limb. As if she wouldn't have noticed.

I turned to my side and rubbed my face, trying to clear those almost-dead, worst-case scenario images from my brain.

So, instead of those, of course, I got a flashback of her ass. Not just the sight of it, but the feel—in my hand, and in my lap.

Christ, I was getting hard just thinking about it. Which was messed up. But probably better than popping wood while she was sobbing in my arms. That would have been bad.

With a sigh, I reached down and cupped myself, let my hand squeeze my cock, halfway between trying to get it down and just enjoying it. I hadn't gotten turned on by a woman in forever. So of course it was the traumatized one sleeping in my bed who'd do it.

How freaking messed up was that?

With another sigh, I tugged at my balls…and stilled.

My eyes opened to find both dogs alert, ears lifted, staring toward my bedroom.

I tilted my head and listened.

After a few minutes, they settled again, but I couldn't manage it.

It was going to be a long night.

9

CHRISTA

*I*t took me a few seconds to figure out where I was and then to remember how I'd gotten here.

Something sharp and frenzied kicked around in my chest—panic, fear, a yawning black hole of *Oh God, what have I done?*—only to be replaced by mortification when I realized that I was buck naked under these blankets.

As I was about to pull the covers over my head and hide out for the duration, I spotted the stack of folded clothes just inside the closed bedroom door.

Micah.

Suddenly, a fresh bout of emotion swamped me—a mix of excitement and curiosity and tenderness at the things he'd done, all balanced by wariness. He was a stranger, after all. And I was stuck here in his home. I came out of this wave with tears in my eyes.

This was overwhelm like I'd never felt in my life. Shock, probably, from almost dying and getting literally torn from my car just in the nick of time. What a day.

My eye landed on the neatly-folded pile of clothes again and I had to work hard not to break down and cry. No. No, I wasn't letting any of that crap turn me into a slushy pile of emotion. The thing I'd hold onto here—the thing that mattered —was that I was apparently the luckiest woman on earth. And I planned to live like it.

Full of excitement, I went to get out of bed and just stopped myself from collapsing on the floor.

Once I got my footing, I made my way to the door slowly, like an old lady—except not Gran, who was absurdly spry—I struggled stiffly into the clothing. Every movement involved testing the body part first. Neck, back, arms, chest, and places I hadn't realized could ache, like the side of my waist. I felt like I'd been bulldozed in the night.

My need to pee made my slow pace feel like a particularly sadistic brand of torture.

Clad in black long underwear, which I'd had to fold over at the sleeves and waist and legs, though it was tight around my boobs and butt and thighs, I stuck my head out the door.

Coffee. Oh my God, that smelled good.

And it confirmed what I'd decided moments before—I was, in fact, the luckiest woman alive.

Quickly, I slipped into the bathroom where I sank onto the toilet with great difficulty, rose with even more, then rubbed some toothpaste on my teeth, and washed my puffy face with ice cold water. My underwear and bra were nowhere to be seen. Okay. I wouldn't be embarrassed about the fact that he'd picked up my panties. Or about walking out there braless.

Another scent slid under the door. Bacon. Luckiest. Ever. My mouth watered. If anything would get me to leave this room and face the big man who'd saved my life, it was bacon.

Okay. Here goes. I took a breath in, opened the door, and almost tripped on the ill-matched pair of dogs—Bear and Brownie.

"Told you to give her space!" Micah's voice was gruffer in the morning. Was he annoyed that I was there? Had he gotten any sleep? I shouldn't have taken his bed. Swamped with guilt, I avoided looking at the messy sofa—avoided looking up at all—turned the corner…

And ran into hot, hard man-chest.

His hands came out to steady me, lingering on my shoulders before setting me back, gently.

"Sorry," I mumbled.

"How you feeling?"

"Good." I forced a smile and met his eyes.

"You're full of shit."

I let the smile drop. "You got me."

He lifted his chin toward the sofa. "Sit. I'll bring you breakfast."

"No. I need to get home. You've done way too m—"

"Girls. Herd her to the sofa." He turned to the stove and my eyes traveled down his top half. Dear God, he was muscular. His naked back wasn't just big, but hard-looking, with indentations where I'd never actually seen them before. I looked down to his butt in olive green cargo shorts, and down.

"Oh! I'm—"

I blinked at his legs: what I could see of one thick thigh, sprinkled with dark hair went on to a sturdy knee and a finely-chiseled calf, ending in a dark grey slipper. On the other side, what looked like a black stocking encased his thigh below his shorts, a space-age metal contraption emerging from the bottom. He had a prosthetic leg. I got that. I understood it, but it didn't compute with what had happened last night.

"How'd you do all th—" My hand flew to my mouth to stop me from saying whatever stupid crap I'd been about to say. And then, because he kept his back to me, I said it anyway. "You carried me up a mountain last night."

His ribs expanded a little and he glanced over his shoulder at me, expression blank. "Sure did."

"With a, um, prosthetic leg."

"Yeah."

"What are you? A freaking superhero or something?"

Though I hadn't meant it as a joke, my

question surprised him into laughing. Or something close to it. A choked huff of a sound. "No. But adrenaline'll help you through some pretty crazy shit."

"So that was all adrenaline? None of it was skill? Or superhuman strength?" I pointed vaguely at his excessive array of muscles.

He put down the fork with which he'd prodded at the bacon, and turned to face me. "I don't let it slow me down."

Apparently not. I shook my head. "Who *are* you?"

"Told you. Name's Micah."

"You wouldn't tell me if you were a secret special agent operative person, would you?"

"Nope." His smile, when he handed me a coffee, was a special kind of magic—like squiggly-belly, juddery-heart kind of magic. It made me both excited and anxious at once. I should get out of here before I did something stupid. Like *right* now. I glanced at the stove. Or maybe after I'd gotten some of that bacon.

The coffee, in a thick, bright orange mug that said **Powered by Stihl**, warmed my hands.

"Cream in the fridge. Sugar's right there." He pointed to a bag on the counter. "Then go sit. I've got news."

I went for both cream and sugar, hyper-aware of how close he was in this tiny kitchen space. Then, just as I'd opened my mouth to offer to help with breakfast, he pointed at the couch again. "Please."

I got the feeling he was handling me the way he handled his dogs—kindly and calmly, but with absolute authority.

"News? What news?"

"Turn around."

I turned and blinked at the room, then focused on the windows. "Shit." Snow poured from the sky onto a landscape already coated in it. "They've cleared the roads, right? I've got to get home. Gran'll—"

"Called the county. Nobody's going anywhere today. Pretty sure I couldn't make it down the mountain anyway, even with my plow."

"I need to call Gran. I can't leave her alone for Christmas. She'll be—"

"She called, actually."

I stared.

"Told me not to wake you. Said she and Gus were just fine and you'd better not do anything foolish." He gave a half-smile. "Scary lady."

Right. Okay.

I nodded and hobbled to the sofa, where I collapsed with a groan and not an ounce of grace. I chose to stare out the window, rather than face the man I was apparently stuck with until further notice. He wouldn't be happy at the intrusion.

Shit. I took a sip and glanced at him. "Wow, this is good coffee."

He grinned, lifting those high cheekbones

higher and carving fine creases around his eyes. Damn, he was handsome. I wondered what he'd look like without the beard and then, because I couldn't help it, I glanced down at his legs again.

"Want the good news, too?"

My eyes flew back up to meet his. Did I?

10

MICAH

"All right." Christa didn't look like she trusted whatever I was about to tell her.

"Still got power, phone's working, wood, and food for days."

"Days?" Had she gone a little pale? "How long…"

"Storm's not letting up anytime soon."

"Aren't you annoyed to have an unexpected guest?"

"No." I turned back to the kitchen to hide my surprise. Annoyed? Jesus, no. Was she annoyed to be here? Of course she was. She had plans for the holiday, friends and family to spend it with. I had my girls and some paperwork I'd put off all year.

"What would you be doing, if I weren't here right now?"

"Uh, chores, I guess."

"Can I help?"

"No." And because that sounded pretty shitty,

even to my own ears, I offered a bone. "Dug around in the freezer and pulled out a couple chickens to roast."

"A couple?"

"You, me, and the girls. Four mouths to feed."

"So…" When she didn't finish her sentence, I glanced back at her. She'd dropped her head back on the sofa and sat staring at the ceiling, coffee in one hand, the other arm wrapped protectively around her chest. "Holy. Shit."

"What?"

"Just thought of something that happened last night."

Oh no. Did I sleepwalk? Say something wrong? Yell out some crazy shit? I tensed and waited.

"Before the…accident." Over and over again, my thoughts stuttered on that moment when she and the car had separated.

She swallowed audibly, remembering, probably, what it had felt like to be trapped by that seatbelt. The shock of almost dying. Of living through it. I knew that feeling and it wasn't all flowers and smiley faces.

"The *stupid* work party. Oh, my God, I can't believe I forgot all about that."

"What happened?"

"Jonathan. My boss. Ex. Ex-boss. What an absolute jerk." She covered her face with her hands and started shaking. It wasn't until she looked up again that I realized she was laughing, not crying. "I should've left the second I got there. Apparently, the stupid thing was cancelled and I had no idea. He didn't even tell me until I'd been there for, like half an hour, in that dress. He was wasted. The creep pulled out his... He grabbed my..." She cleared her throat. "My breast."

I'd kill him.

"I kneed him in the crotch and took off."

"You're laughing about this."

"Better than tears."

"Guy lives up there, right? Jonathan... Crandle?" At her nod, I threw down the kitchen towel and stalked to the closet to grab my boots. The asshole had to be stuck up at his place, as surely as we were. I'd tear him apart.

"Hey."

Limb from fucking limb.

"What are you..." She stood and watched me struggle to put on my boots. "You're not going up there."

"Sure am."

"What? No way."

"You're okay with what he did? Just want him to get away with it?" I was breathing hard, my vision dark at the edges. Should have known that a guy who drove like he did would hurt women. Dickless fuck.

"He didn't get away with it. I kneed him. In the balls!"

"Yeah?" I reached for my coat and slid it on. "I'm gonna finish the job."

"You can't do that. What does that even mean, anyway? Are you planning to—" She stood and ran to the door. "Hey! Stop. Stop it!"

"Guy's a shitbag." I put out an arm to set her out of my way and she wrapped herself around it like a vine.

"Yes. Yes, he is." Her voice was low. Urgent. "And if you ignore me right now, *you're* an asshole."

"I want to hurt him." The words came out, sharp and ugly. I imagined hitting him, could feel the crunch of bone against my knuckles, could smell the blood.

"You can't." Her eyes flicked between mine and her hand tightened on my arm, hanging on me. "Stay here. With me."

Brownie whined from where she stood, alert in front of the fire, her eyebrows twitching as she watched.

"Look, Micah. It was awful. He's a creep. But, because of you, I can honestly say that my night got better." She stepped into my space and snagged me with her dark intensity. "I mean, I almost fell off a cliff, but then you *saved* me. Do you know how amazing it is to almost die? To be here when—" She glanced down at my leg and back up, something so familiar on her face that all I could think was, *I know this woman. I* know *her.* "Yeah, I guess you probably get it, Micah. Right now, I feel *alive*. Exhausted, in pain, shell-shocked and freaked out that my car's gone. It's probably polluting your beautiful mountainside. I can't believe I have to figure out a job situation and I'm worried that my presence is annoying as hell to you…but I'm *alive*. Luckiest woman in the world." Her lopsided grin was *fascinating*. "Because of *you*. *You*. And I don't want anything to happen to you. Including hurting yourself by hurting him. He's not worth it, Micah. But *you* are."

Her words felled me, twisted me up in knots, made me feel bigger and stronger.

"You get it, Micah? We may not know each other, but…" She put her hands to her face and shook her head. "Crap, you're gonna think I'm batshit crazy, but here it is." Her intensity was almost blinding when she looked at me. Her inner strength superhuman. "Right here, right now, right this minute, you're the most important person in my life. You risked your life to save mine."

I opened my mouth to protest, but she put up a hand to stop me. "No biggie, I know. The point is, if you went to prison for beating that asshole up, I'd never forgive myself, ever. For involving you, for telling you what he did, for letting you go up there and do things you'd regret."

Oh. I could see that.

"So, please. Please stay here. Okay?"

I swallowed and stepped back, taking her in, from the high shine in her eyes to the bright pink circles on her cheeks, then down to the quick rise and fall of her chest.

I blinked. "Yeah." The need to hurt faded to a tingling in my fingers and toes—all four limbs feeling the exact the same thing, as if I hadn't left one back on that roadside in Afghanistan. "I'm sorry."

"Don't be. You are an ama—" Her lips pressed together and she swallowed, then shook her head. "How about that bacon?"

11

CHRISTA

I stood by the front door watching Micah stomp to the kitchen in his boots and coat. His brow was creased, his mouth tight, his face as darkly dangerous as the chasm I'd nearly lost my life to.

What the hell had I gotten myself into here? One jerk up the mountain trying to grab my boob and this guy flying off the handle at the drop of a hat. In all fairness, he had good reason to lose it. I just didn't want him to ruin his life over it.

I followed his movements for a few more seconds, still wary that he'd blow right out the door if I moved.

"You taking off that coat or do I have to stand here forever?"

He stilled, back to me. "Can't." His head dropped. Were his shoulders shaking?

"Why not?"

"'Cause then you'll see that I forgot to put on

a shirt and long pants under this and realize what a douchebag I am."

"Yeah, well…" I broke out into a grin, fighting an actual laugh. "You had a shirt on when you saved my life last night. Guess I'll let this one slide."

He threw me a funny look, unzipped his big coat and put it away, then grabbed his slippers, set them on the floor by the bench, where he removed his boots, and replaced them with the slippers.

Watching his precise movements, it occurred to me that he had to keep his place neat or it might trip him up. I hadn't been in any condition to notice last night, aside from a general impression of small and dark and rustic. As I took in the details, now, it became clear that rustic didn't necessarily mean rough-hewn. In fact, the light coming in made the place downright bright and it was remarkably clean and…fresh.

By the time he'd put on his slippers and looked up to meet my eyes, the humor I'd felt earlier had morphed into something else. Not any one clear emotion, but a mess of feelings in my belly and chest, so mixed up it wasn't clear if I'd end up in laughter or tears, or maybe doing something completely off the wall, like pounding the floor.

What would this morning have been like, if I'd made it home last night and awakened in my own bed?

After being attacked and leaving my job? Bad. Really, really bad.

He went to the kitchen, where he lit the stove, grabbed something from the fridge, and went to work.

I took another minute to look around.

This looked like pretty new construction, actually, with built-in details that had to be specially-made for him. The bench beside the front door, for example, and the shoe cubby beneath it. The kitchen was entirely made of smooth, streamlined wood. White pine? I could tell you the weight of a sheet of card stock from ten feet away, but lumber? I had no idea. The dining table was the same type of construction—sturdy and simple. Whitewash the whole thing and it would look like that modern Swedish stuff people went crazy over.

The dark, plain grey sofa was probably the oldest thing in the room, aside from a rag rug in front of the fire, and the wood stove itself.

I liked it—the high ceiling, the warm, knotty wood, the feeling that it belonged up here on the mountain, blended in, unlike the ostentatious eyesore I'd gone to last night.

"Eggs okay?"

I blinked. "Um, yeah. But you don't have to—"

"You like 'em scrambled?"

"Yes." I watched him work for a few minutes. "So… What do you do for a living?"

"Arborist."

My brows flew up. Man, the guy wasn't kidding about not letting that leg impede him. "You climb trees and stuff?"

"I do. You?"

"No. No, I do not climb trees."

"Should try it. Quite the view from up there. And it's kind of a rush."

"Yeah, well, I've had my share of rushes this week."

"What's your job?"

I flushed. Oh, that was probably what he'd meant, rather than whether or not I climbed trees.

"Marketing Manager for a local company. Project 54. We create Integration Platforms for —" Anxiety hit me like a punch to the gut. "Actually, I don't have a job, do I?" Something a lot like relief filled the empty places in the wake of that wave of panic. "I'm currently seeking opportunities in Marketing and Communications. Preferably at a female-owned company." My own, one day.

He eyed me for a few seconds, without speaking, probably checking me for signs of an imminent breakdown.

"It's strangely freeing, actually, not to work for that creep anymore."

"I'll bet."

"Investor profit. I'm so tired of pretending to care about that soulless crap."

He made a pained face. "Can't imagine." He walked to the built-in dining table, set two plates down, then made another trip with the coffee. Did he have a limp? Not really. A long gait, heavy footsteps. Nothing I would have noticed out in the world. "You okay to sit here, or you prefer the couch?"

"Oh," I started, guiltily. I'd been staring at his legs, hadn't I? Was I distilling the man to a disability, rather than the person inside? I wouldn't look below the belt again. Wouldn't think about it. "I'm coming."

"Be right back." He disappeared into his bedroom and re-emerged wearing long pants and buttoning a flannel shirt, his face a little flushed. He looked up and met my eyes briefly before settling across from me. "Sorry."

"Oh." For catching me staring at his half-naked body? I picked up my silverware, but he didn't move.

"For…" He pointed awkwardly at the door behind me. "That, I mean."

"Oh." I put down the fork and knife with a clang. "But, you risked your life to save mine. Whatever *thing* you have that pushed you to do that…" Excessive testosterone or muscles or *insane* amounts of courage. "I'm guessing is the same instinct that made you fly off the handle and want to pay that jerk back for what he did to me. I get it. But *I* hurt him already." I couldn't help a self-satisfied smirk at the memory of Jonathan sinking to the floor with a groan, rolling into a ball, calling me a bitch. "I'll probably file some official thing someplace. A police report or whatever. For posterity. Despite the *he said she said* thing. But…" I caught his eyes and held them, needing him to get it. "I appreciate the sentiment." I picked up the fork, ready to be done with this, but also needing him to understand that he was—he'd always be the stranger who saved my life. A hero. "And all of this. Bed, food, clothes. I mean…"

"Stop now." He sounded gruff and his cheekbones had gone a painful-looking red. "Please?"

"Okay."

"Will you just eat?"

I eyed the absurd mountain of food on my plate. "I'll try."

12

MICAH

What am I supposed to do with this woman?

Laid out on my sofa, talking on the phone to her grandmother, the cops, and then her insurance company, she was as out of place in my home as an...aardvark or something. I'd be more comfortable if a grizzly showed up and took a dump in my bed.

She handled the red tape shit well, especially considering she'd dangled over that precipice less than a dozen hours ago. Sure would be nice to talk on the phone that easily, instead of turning into an idiot every time I had to answer questions or give my social security number. I'd bet the person she was talking to had no idea that the confident, ballsy lady on this end of the line was laid out on my sofa in worn-out oversized long johns, her body bruised to hell, scratching a dog under the chin with one hand and taking notes with the other.

My place smelled different with her in it, it looked different, too. Smaller, shabbier, maybe a little brighter.

Gotta get out of here.

I put on my boots and coat, grabbed my spare work gloves, and waved at her on the way out.

Outside, the blizzard was *on*. Hadn't seen one like this in a couple years. I had enough wood cut, which was good, since I didn't really want to be chopping in this weather. I pulled my hat down and threw the hood up over it, then went to check the property for downed trees, wires, that kind of stuff. I had a generator, but the hum of its engine made me crazy. As loud as it got when I worked, chainsaw in hand, I liked things quiet at home.

It was why I'd built up here, away from everything, against the advice of doctors and physical therapists and shrinks. Kept things simple. No rules to follow. Just mine and Mother Nature's.

Bear's, when she decided she wanted something.

I paused at the sound of Christa's voice carrying through the thick front door, expecting the usual jolt of irritation at an intrusion.

Nothing. Hm. Maybe it was the Christmas spirit, or something, telling me to simmer on the annoyance with others or I'd turn into Scrooge.

I spent the next hour or so tromping around

the woods, keeping myself as busy as I could. I even went up to the next rise to see if I could catch a glimpse of that douche-bag's place, but the snow made visibility impossible.

It wasn't until I went into my workshop and flicked the light switch that I realized the power was out. Was she freezing her ass off alone in there? Phone line was probably down, too and my cell wouldn't work without the internet. I hoofed it back to the cabin and hesitated with my hand on the doorknob. Should I knock?

No. Jesus.

Slowly, to give her a chance to—whatever it was she might need to do before I walked in on her—I opened the door, glanced at the empty couch, and had a moment's relief, followed quickly by panic. Gone.

No, dumbshit. She can't be.

My eyes flew to the bathroom door, which was open, then to my bedroom—also open, but not all the way. I took two steps before I realized I couldn't go charging in there like a bull in a china shop. She was probably resting. God knew she'd need it after last night. Christ, she'd probably need therapy. Could take years to get over a trauma like that.

The dogs, who'd shown no interest in going out into the storm with me, were nowhere to be seen. With her, then. Probably.

Lucky bitches.

Okay, then.

I turned to look at the wall clock. Two in the afternoon. I should get those chickens going soon. Unless…would she sleep straight through till tomorrow?

"Micah?" Apparently not.

I stilled. "Uh. Yeah?"

"I couldn't find your ibuprofen. You think I could have some?"

"Course." I went to the cupboard where I kept stuff like that—above the fridge. Putting stuff up high was one of those weird leftover things from growing up in a house with lots of kids. Pointless now, but something I still did.

I grabbed a bottle of water from my stockpile under the sink—no running water without power —snagged the ibuprofen, and went into my room.

13

CHRISTA

I swallowed the pills and sank back into the pillows with a grunt.

"How am I hurting so much?"

I expected him to ignore me and walk out, but his footsteps stopped. "Where?"

"Oh, God. Everywhere?"

He gave me a *go on* kind of look.

Slowly, one muscle at a time, I took inventory. "Neck. Kinda jammed on one side. Chest and ribs, all through here."

"Seatbelt." His eyes scanned me, from top to bottom, and I could only imagine what he was thinking. I'd been called all kinds of names in my life. Like, why did so many dudes feel obliged to lean out their car windows to inform me that I was fat? They were the jerks driving looking at me. I was just minding my own business. And then there were the compliments that weren't. Just a couple weeks back, I'd been out with a friend when a bartender had leaned in, smarmy smile on his face and said, "I just love a confident big girl." It hadn't felt like flattery. Just a sharp little reminder that I wasn't somehow normal, or the *right* size. If he'd said it without the big, it would've been another story.

We didn't even finish our drinks before leaving.

This guy, with his chiseled abs and unbelievable strength, who could climb freaking mountains despite a pretty extreme physical impairment, was probably wondering how I'd let myself go like this. But I hadn't. This wasn't me with a few extra pounds, this was—*me*. Period. From the time I'd hit puberty, I was just…round.

And I was fine with the way I looked. It was the jerks around me who had issues with it.

"Where else?"

I threw him a grumpy side-eye, and felt immediately contrite when I realized how hard I was breathing. Because, yeah, I'd just worked myself up over something he had nothing to do with. "Um." I cleared my throat, embarrassed and more than a little freaked out at how easily I'd taken off into my head. "Upper back's a mess."

"Roll over." The words were quiet; an order. They sliced through every one of my thoughts, landing me in this room, in this bed, alone with this man. "If you want."

Our eyes met. His didn't contain an ounce of

the stupid crap people threw my way because of *their* relationships with *my* body. His face was placid, judgement-free, as if to say, *You're hurt. I can help you.*

It calmed something in me, quieted the worries. I struggled onto my front.

He mumbled that he'd be right back and I lay there for a good thirty seconds.

When he returned, he stopped abruptly. "Oh, uh… Maybe you should…"

"Hm?"

"I forgot about your shirt."

I craned my neck to look as he held up a tube of cream. Was he blushing? The guy who'd cradled me last night, while I sobbed in his arms? Naked?

"Oh, right. Can't reach."

He remained frozen.

"Hang on." I was halfway up when his hand landed on my shoulder.

"Stay."

That wasn't supposed to get me worked up, was it? Being talked to like a dog or something. And yet, somehow, that one word did just that. Or maybe it was his touch, warm and heavy through the worn cotton of the shirt. *His* shirt.

Breathless, I dropped back to my front and waited for what felt like forever. He finally shoved my shirt up, managing not to touch my bare skin at all.

"Maybe, uh…"

I glanced back to see him gesturing vaguely at my back, the visible parts of his face so red he appeared sunburned.

"Oh." Awkwardly, I lifted my top half up so he could get the shirt above my shoulders and almost all the way off. The fabric grazed my nipples and I dropped back with an *oof*, hyper-aware of my breasts, flattened to the bed now, the sides no doubt perfectly visible.

After a few long seconds, he sank to the bed beside me, his weight making me roll into him. Would he shift back? Should I?

Neither of us moved until he opened the tube of cream. I braced myself for that first cold squirt. It never came. He must have rubbed it between his hands, because when he finally massaged me, there was nothing but warmth. And somehow, he knew exactly where I needed it.

His strong, rough fingers carved out a semicircle around first one aching shoulder blade, then the other. He kneaded at me, pressing at a knot to loosen it, then moving on to the next. I let out a sound, then another, until finally what emerged from my mouth was a long, low, constant groan of pleasure-pain.

The man was a miracle worker, those hands some kind of magic.

Over and over, he worked at me, his movements deep and slow. At some point, our breathing synchronized, gasped mint-laced inhalations flowing into long, heaving exhalations.

He leaned forward to pluck gently at my neck, his chest close enough to warm my back, though not quite touching it, and all I could think was, *Do it. Get on top. Straddle me. Cover me with that impossibly strong body. Show me what it can do.*

Who the hell was I? I'd put this man out, forced myself into the solitude he clearly sought, and now, to top it all off, while he worked his ass off to heal me, I objectified him.

Goosebumps, which he couldn't possibly *not* see, ran out from every place he touched with his hands, making my skin doubly sensitive, alive.

By the time he pulled away, I was a sweaty, guilty, squirming mess. Despite the sore muscles— or maybe because of them—I felt swollen, pumped full of blood and a strange sort of need.

"That good?" he asked, gruffly. I imagined a tinge of resentment in those words, as if he'd meant to add *enough* at the end, and just held back.

"Amazing." My voice came out lower than I'd intended.

He didn't get up, didn't move and, though I wanted a look at his face, I didn't dare turn around, couldn't burst this bubble by opening my eyes.

After a long, uncomfortable, hyper-aware handful of seconds, his hands returned to my shoulders and I tensed. *This is it. He'll touch me differently now, take advantage in a way that I welcome, instead of how that Jonathan jackass did it last night.*

Only it wasn't like that, of course. Because guys like him didn't take advantage. And, probably, he didn't even want me that way, which made my own fantasies absurd and more than a little misplaced.

Roughly, in a purely practical way, he grasped at the shirt and pulled it over my back. When one of his pinkies skimmed the soft side of my breast, lighting up my nerves like a Christmas tree, it was purely accidental. Obviously.

Once I was fully covered, those big hands landed at the base of my back. So quickly I must have imagined it, his thumbs brushed under the cotton, along my spine up, then down.

He let out a long, shaky breath, tightened his grip briefly around my waist, and stomped out of the room, leaving me alone to figure out what the hell had just happened.

14

MICAH

*C*hrista didn't leave my bed for the rest of the day, which was a relief. I shouldn't have done that, shouldn't have touched her at all. But that last bit—the squeeze at the end... Fuck. When was the last time I put my hands around a woman's waist?

Years. My last leave, in fact.

I shoved the chickens into the hot oven, shut the door, and stepped back, clenching and unclenching fingers that couldn't seem to lose the feel of her. Not just the softness of her skin—as foreign to a man like me as some wild animal to a city person—but the ripe swell of her hips.

Even now, hours later, I got hard just thinking about it.

While rubbing her back, I'd stared at her nape —slender and...not weak, exactly, but dainty or something. Vulnerable, in need of protection. I'd fought the urge to press my lips to that defenseless spot, and then, as if that wouldn't freak her out, to add my teeth to the mix.

Jesus, how would she have reacted? Especially after the shit she'd gone through last night—not just in her car, but with her asshole boss?

A surge of possessiveness rocked me, tightening my muscles, making me tense and angry and, fuck me, just a little hornier.

Wrong. Completely wrong.

How would she respond to the unwanted advances of a man like me?

She wouldn't have to kick me in the nuts. Because I wouldn't touch her again. Okay, I'd rub her back if she asked me, but I wouldn't give in like I'd done with that last squeeze.

Something shifted in the other room—her or one of the dogs, who'd laid down on the floor beside the bed—and, rather than wait around to see how badly I'd fucked up with that move, I rushed to put my boots on, opened the door, and whistled for the dogs.

The cold hit me right off the bat—a welcome smack to the face. Good. Maybe the girls and I would camp out here tonight.

It'd probably be safer.

But, Jesus, couldn't I just get a grip? She was injured, for God's sake. Not begging me to fuck her.

"Girls!" Clearly, they didn't want to leave her either. After a few seconds—probably a long, drawn-out stretch, Brownie slunk into the room, yawning, but no Bear. "Bear!" When, finally, the little hairball joined me at the door, I could've sworn she threw me an irritated look. Like, *Why'd you pull me away from the warm lady in the bed?* "Come on. Out." With all the attitude of one of my sisters, they followed me outside.

I opened my mouth to tell Christa where we were going and closed it. We weren't a couple. This wasn't some domestic, "Honey, just headed out for a bit" moment.

Instead, I shut the door and stomped through the two feet of snow toward my workshop, in search of something to do with my hands.

Checking my equipment would have to do, since the weather barred pretty much everything else. I grabbed my rope bag and yanked out a long coil of rope, along with the mechanical prusiks I used to facilitate movement up and down trees.

Bear started whining for dinner an hour or so later. I'd checked all my rigging, gone over lanyards, carabiners, harnesses, and ropes. It was almost dark out and I'd need to turn the stove off anyway, so I had to get back to the cabin. The problem wasn't that I didn't want to, it was that I wanted it too much.

So, maybe my sisters had been right. Maybe I did need to get out more often, talk to people, see old friends, meet women.

What about the woman in my house?

Off-limits, idiot. That was Cindy's voice talking

in my head—my youngest sibling. *You want a woman on even footing. Not one who's dependent on you for everything.*

She was right, damn it.

I trudged back to the house, the girls dogging my footsteps, barely taking the time to pee before rushing through the hard-driving snow toward the cabin. Dinner wasn't something they took lightly.

On the porch, I wiped the girls down, knocked the snow off my boots, and peered at the windows. Was there light on in there? Shit, I hadn't thought to leave her with a flashlight or candles or anything.

I opened the door and the dogs shot inside like furry, wet cannons.

"Oh, hey!" Christa giggled "Hey Bear! Hey Brownie!"

I forced myself to concentrate on my boots for a good ten seconds longer. When I finally dared to look at her, I could see her face flush, even in the dark of the candle-lit cabin. My neck prickled with heat of its own.

"You all right?"

She nodded. "Like a new person."

I nodded and sank to the bench, where I pulled on my slippers.

Play it cool. I stood, noting that she'd taken the chickens out and covered them with foil.

"So—"

"Do you think—"

We both stopped and let out awkward little laughs.

"Go ahead."

"No. No, ladies first." I cringed at those words, picturing the precise look on Cindy's face if she heard me saying that. "Or guest first." Or something. *Jesus, Graham. Get it together.*

She broke through the silence. "Is that what I am? Your guest?"

"Well, of course."

"Unwanted, though." A smile played around the edges of her mouth, but her eyes looked unsure.

"No." *Definitely* not.

She shrugged. "Well, then unexpected, at least."

"Maybe." And then, because I couldn't let her hang like that, I went on. "But appreciated."

"Yeah?"

It was my turn to shrug—which made me feel like a kid again. A stupid teenager, always skirting around things, unwilling to commit. I immediately regretted it. I opened my mouth to say something reassuring. Like an adult, damn it. But my eyes were distracted by the amber glow of the bourbon bottle and—coward that was—I used it to get out of this conversation.

"Want a drink?"

Her brows rose. "Is that safe? With all the painkillers?"

"You take a lot of ibuprofen? I mean, before this?"

She shook her head.

"You'll be fine."

I went to the cupboard and grabbed two glasses, poured a couple fingers of booze into each, and glanced at her. "Ice?"

"You having any?"

"No."

"That's okay."

I handed her the drink and waited for her to sit on the sofa before following her.

"What time is it?"

I checked the wall clock. "Almost five."

She looked surprised. "Thought it was later. Still not dinnertime yet."

"We can eat whenever you want." I threw a look at the two mutts watching us like spectators at a tennis match. "The girls think now would be good. I'll debone some chicken for their dinner."

"Oh, well, we can—"

"It is a little early, even for them." I lifted my arm to take a sip of my drink, but she stopped me.

"Hey. Um. Cheers."

"Oh. Yeah." I put my glass out, eyes trained on it. "Cheers."

"Here's to, uh...to spending Christmas with a..." She sucked in a shaky breath, drawing my eyes right to her face. "Handsome stranger."

15

CHRISTA

*M*icah went absolutely still, which would have been comical, given that the hand holding his drink was suspended straight out in front of him. Like what I'd said had stopped time. Like we were two flies caught in the amber light of this room, flash frozen by this moment of complete embarrassment.

Geez, Christa. Maybe try not to come on to the moody man-bear again. He was so clearly ready to be rid of me that it would have been comical. If the rejection didn't feel so bad.

I pulled my glass away, breaking the spell in the process, and slugged back more bourbon than I'd intended. It burned a hot path straight to my belly and, despite the new tension, eased my joints a little. The pain didn't go away, exactly. If anything, it burned hotter for a few seconds, but I somehow didn't mind it as much.

Ready to shove that awkward moment behind

me, I took another sip. This one went down easier in the shadow of the first. Good. Maybe if I drank enough, I wouldn't notice the way he avoided me. I could pass out and wake up and, if all went smoothly, tomorrow the snow would stop and I could find someone to come up here and get me.

"So, where are you from, Christa?"

I couldn't help the surprised look I threw at Micah. Was he actually making small talk?

"Um. Seattle. I mean, my family's from up here, but…I just moved back."

"To be with your grandmother."

"Yeah. My granddad died a couple years ago. And she had a stroke a few months back. Couldn't leave her here. On her own, you know?"

"Yeah."

"What about you?"

He looked a question at me.

"You always live here? In this cabin?"

"Oh. No. No. Bought the land a while back. Been in the cabin a couple years now."

"And before that?"

"Army."

"Is that where—" Crap. I hadn't intended to go there. It wasn't any of my business where he'd lost his leg. And probably wasn't something he wanted to talk about, either. I opened my mouth, ready to backpedal, but apparently, after downing his bourbon in one shot, he had other ideas.

When he stood and walked to the little

kitchen area, I almost followed him to… I don't know. Maybe apologize for prying? Maybe tell him to forget about it. Or, I could lock myself in the bathroom until the roads cleared. It was big enough, and there was a little seat in there…

I didn't expect him to grab the bottle and fill both our glasses before settling back onto the sofa beside me. A little closer, even, than he'd been before.

"What you humming?"

"Was I?" Probably. I did that when I was nervous. "Oh. A Christmas song, maybe."

"Which one?"

I hummed low and then stopped, flushing even redder than I'd been before, and hid my face. "It's ridiculous."

"Why?"

"It's the worst Christmas song."

"Lemme guess. Um, the drum one."

"No! That one's good."

He snorted. "Okay… That two front teeth one."

"*No!* It's Good King Wenceslas, okay? That's the one I'm humming."

His lips turned down at the corners. "Can't say I've heard of it."

"You know, deep and crisp and even."

"It's a Christmas song about pizza?"

"Nooooo, *silly*, it's…"

He changed, subtly. I couldn't figure out how, but something about the shift made me go very still, blinking at eyes that focused hard on my mouth. *He's going to kiss me.*

He didn't.

Kiss me. Do it. Let me feel those hard-looking lips on mine, put those hands on me again.

"I'll tell you the truth, Christa, because you seem like a nice person and…" He shut his eyes with a sharp sigh, took a sip, and turned away. "I wouldn't want to get your hopes up."

"My hopes?" I shook my head and opened my mouth to deny that I'd had any hopes.

"I spent about two years on the street."

I straightened, my skin suddenly blazing hot. "On the—"

"Homeless."

"Oh. Okay?"

"And it's not 'cause I don't have family or any shit like that. I do. I have parents who love me and four sisters. They all love me. They wanted me to move in with them. They live an hour from here and I almost never see 'em."

He paused. Did he want me to say something? Because there wasn't really anything, was there? His life was so different from mine. Who was I to judge or assume or even comment?

And what did he think my hopes were up about, exactly? Those words of his wound a thread of irritation through me.

"I chose to stay out on my own. In the woods, mostly, though I slept on a few city streets." He threw a side eye my way. "Seattle once, actually."

Oh, my God. Had I walked by him at some point? Had I given him money as I stomped down the sidewalk on my way to work? I racked my brain, trying to remember if I'd ever seen him before.

"Lasted about five hours in the city before I had to turn around and leave again."

"Why?" I whispered.

"You ever feel trapped in your life?"

"Uh." Had I? I thought about it, hard, since he was giving me honesty, telling me real things, and he deserved a real answer. "Yeah. Yeah, I guess. I felt trapped in my job, actually. Project 54. But there's not that much work around here, so I stuck with it. Before, too, I guess. In relationships, even. My last boyfriend wanted to get married and I didn't really want to, but…" Whoa. Was it him or the booze bringing this stuff out? Because I'd never, ever thought of myself as being trapped with my ex before. Even when I broke off the wedding, I'd made it more about our differing priorities than anything else.

"But?"

"I agreed to anyway. What kind of jerk wouldn't want what he was offering, right?"

"Why didn't you want it?"

"Honestly?" I met his eyes, feeling brazen, suddenly, with my secrets out. "I loved him like a friend. He was funny and warm, comfortable. All of those things." I swallowed. "But I wasn't attracted to him anymore." Unlike Micah, who

I'd spent less than 24 hours with. This guy, I was attracted to with every hair, every pore, every nerve in my body. "Maybe never was."

"Why were you with him, then?"

"I'd say laziness, but I don't think it was that." I eyed him—big shoulders, straight back, everything solid and sure. "I'd had a run of jerks before. Guys always looking for greener grass, or something? Like I was a stepping stone to some perfect vision they had. Fine for a while, but not marriage material. And my ex, well, he loved me. Like, *really* loved me. And I figured…" I waited for the answer to come, in a way baffled, again, by my own incomprehensible choices. "I figured he was it for me."

"Except no sex."

Sex. Just hearing the word on this man's lips made my body react—as if to prove how stupid I'd been to think, once upon a time, that maybe I wasn't sexual anymore, because I hadn't been able to get it up for my ex.

"Right."

"And now?"

I huffed out a laugh, ignoring the heavy weight pooling between my thighs. Wetness, I'd bet, although nothing had happened between us. Nothing, I reminded myself. "Well, still no sex."

MICAH

"*S*hame."

"Yeah, well. I promised myself I wouldn't settle again."

"Good. You shouldn't." It came out bossier than intended. But then part of me needed reminding, too. I wouldn't let her settle for someone like me. Someone whose brain didn't always work right, who couldn't quite get a handle on society. Who needed solitude like most people needed water.

"Yes, sir."

Those two words sent a tingling down my spine. Not an Army flashback, I realized after a moment, but something else. Something darker and deeper, older than the military. Something that made my pants a little tight and my belly warm. And then that thing, whatever it was, opened my mouth and pushed words out. "When I was homeless, I dreamed of a woman like you."

Even now. Tell her. Even now, I can't stop thinking about it.

She gasped, the sound barely audible, though it left her mouth open.

"Someone beautiful. Strong, you know?" And then my mouth took off without me. "And smart, with a..." *Idiot.* "*Juicy* body."

"Oh."

"Always into curves like yours." I didn't dare look at her as I continued. "Stuff fantasies are made of."

"Oh, okay."

"I know. You didn't ask me, did you?" I sighed and leaned back into the cushions, rubbing my face hard. What the hell was I doing? Why was I telling her this shit? Probably scare the crap out of her. "You being here." I coughed out a pained little half-laugh. "Kinda throwing me for a loop." I lifted a hand. "My fault, not yours. *My* problem."

She huffed out a laugh and threw me a side-eye that said maybe I was the one throwing her for a loop.

As if she needed one more horny asshole making a play for her.

Even that thought didn't stop me from following some booze-bred urge to put my hand out, palm up, on the sofa. I stared at it, cracked and callused, between us, as though it wasn't even a part of me, but something I put on in the morning, like my leg. For someone who didn't spend all that much time in my head, I suddenly felt like I wasn't inhabiting my body either.

Homeless, wandering, looking at my overly-breakable edges from someplace outside. I'd say hovering in the air above us, except that hand between us was my version of flattening out on the floor, prostrating myself.

She laid her cool palm over mine, slid her fingers between mine, and squeezed. Just that touch and I flew back inside—my person, my soul or something—filling out my flesh to its edges.

And only then could I confront this thing I'd torn open and look at her face again. What I saw shoved the air from my lungs and closed my fingers around her hand, in an unconscious spasm.

"What are we doing?" she asked.

I stroked my thumb along her finger, the only place I could reach without moving our hands and ruining the moment. "I don't know."

I couldn't tear my gaze from her face, so pretty and doll-like, but also flushed and real. Warm and soft. Bright and lively. Her teeth bit into that tender bottom lip, mesmerizing me more surely than any drug I'd tried and rejected. This woman could become an addiction.

One of the dog's collars rattled, bringing me out of my stupor.

"You hungry?"

She blinked, like it'd woken her up, too. "Just a minute." Her eyes flicked down to where our hands acted out all my fantasies. "I don't want this to end."

Those words set off an explosion inside me— excitement, yeah, but also nerves like I rarely got anymore, except when meeting a new client or something.

"This okay?"

"Yeah." She tightened her fingers briefly. "Weird, right?"

"Oh, um—"

"I don't mean you. It's…this. Like, last night I'd never heard of you. And now, I'm…"

What? She was what? I watched her mouth, waiting for the next word like the dogs were waiting for their dinner. When nothing came, I turned fully toward her, bent my head, and kissed her.

Hell. I was like a teenage version of myself, all nerves and excitement, moving so quickly that I smashed my mouth to hers, instead of touching it that first time. I almost pulled away before I realized she was into it. We'd pried our hands apart and hers—both of them—were on me, holding herself steady with my shoulder, but definitely pulling me closer with the one clamped around my neck.

Her little mouth made me hungry—all soft lips and hot breath. I wanted to pull her onto my lap and eat her, but I calmed that beast right the hell down, or shoved it back. Temporarily.

Man, what was it about the taste, the smell,

the feel of a woman? It'd been so long, it was like learning all over again, but I knew how to do this. Like riding a bike or climbing a tree, it was that initial hesitation I had to get over. I grabbed her face with my hands—not too tight, though I couldn't help steadying her, holding her still for my mouth—and I tasted her with my tongue. She let out these gasps; hot, shuddering breaths against me.

"Goddamn." What a sweet talker. "You taste so good."

She'd stop this now, surely. I'd somehow tricked her into thinking I was something I wasn't. It was the savior thing. Being yanked, last minute, from a falling car would do that to a person. Make them want you, or at least feel like they owed you something.

But she didn't stop and I sure as hell wasn't going to make her. Instead, she did what I'd pictured: climbed up and onto her knees, scooted forward, and got on my lap, wrapping her arms around my neck. For a few hot seconds, she leaned back enough to give me a look that I had no idea how to read, her shadowed eyes moving from the top of my head, down, side to side, from one eye to another, then back to my mouth. I let her look, my hands resting lightly on her hips, just waiting.

Wanting.

17

CHRISTA

*G*ood Lord, this man was hot. Not just hot, but sort of…fantasy-worthy. Hard and eager, with hands that demanded, without forcing. The way he watched me watch him right now, like an animal waiting for a sign before going in for the kill.

Going in for the kill? How was I even thinking this crap?

But even when I tried to scoff it away, that feeling remained, of being watched through the glittering eyes of a wary beast. There were layers in the look he gave me—instincts or something— that I could've sworn were predatory, despite the fact that he didn't budge, didn't hold me down. Didn't attack, teeth first.

Whoa. My breath got all crazy just imagining that scenario.

Because, man, the guy could do whatever he

wanted. I'd never met anyone stronger, never had my hands on muscles like these—not bulging like those Instagram assholes who spent every waking hour at the gym or snapping pics of themselves, but thick, supple—real. The man who saved my ass. Literally. And who kissed me like he wanted to eat me.

His hands went to my hips and pressed down, grinding me against him.

Following my own unexpected desires, I leaned in, not to turn over and show him my belly like some kind of prey, but to run my cheek over that beard and the skin above it, to smell his insanely attractive man-smell, to meet him on equal footing, to offer myself up, like the female of his species. Like this was right.

Or something.

Geez, what was with me? I let out a half giggle.

"What?" When he started to turn toward me, I kissed his ear to stop him, nipped it, and ran my lips along the scalding skin below.

"I can't stop thinking of you like a…" I bit his neck and he grunted, the sound a fist reaching inside me to twist up my insides, to set them on fire and push the truth from my mouth. "An animal, or something." I huffed out a nervous laugh, because my words sounded wrong once they were out. Insulting. "Not… Crap." I swayed back to find him watching me, mouth flat, eyes narrowed and wary. I'd said exactly the wrong thing. "I didn't mean—"

"I know what you meant." He smiled. The expression turned the savage beast thing up about a hundred watts, but shoved a sharp wedge between us.

I considered shifting toward him again. He made that impossible by pushing me off him— albeit gently—and rising.

"Let's have dinner." Gone was the wild man I'd wanted to dig into seconds ago. This guy was remote. Had I hurt him? Or just come off like a creep?

"Right." I blinked past a jolt of embarrassment and regret and something like shame, and followed him. Things had been going so well and I'd had to go and ruin it all with my big mouth.

He handed me plates and silverware and I set the table by the side window, then turned and watched him carve the chickens. His hands were deft and capable and now that I'd touched one, I knew for a fact that they had rough, sharp calluses. I unconsciously rubbed my fingers to my own soft palm, wondering again how I could fix the weirdness between us.

"I wasn't fetishizing you." Except maybe I was? Was that what I was doing? Turning him into some bestial fantasy, when he was just an introvert, living on his own? "That wasn't what I meant." Nor did I mean to open my mouth and say that just now. But I could never let things lie.

He stopped cutting and met my eye. "Fetishizing me?"

"Yeah, you know…" Why couldn't I stop talking? Things had gone from really, really good, to slightly awkward, and I was dragging the situation down into unbearable, wasn't I? "The animal thing was a…a compliment. It was good."

"Okay." He ripped off a wing and set it on a serving dish.

"It's just that, while we were kissing, I felt… like…" His brows rose above those light, shimmering eyes and for just a second I wondered if he knew exactly what I meant and was messing with me, letting me shovel my own stupid hole. "*Animalistic.* It was intense for me. I don't usually… It was like we were *both*…wild animals. Like you were dominant…and I was…" Shit, Shut up, Christa. *Shut up!* "Oh, God. What am I talking about?"

His head tilted to the side and he watched me, closely. "You liked it?"

"Well, you know…" I shut my mouth on a string of words he didn't need to hear and I didn't need to say. "Yes. I liked it very much."

After a last assessing look, he nodded once and went back to carving, the knife glinting in the low light, his movements so freaking precise, so well-practiced, something an awful lot like fear twisted in my belly. I glanced out the window at the eerie blue light. It was still coming down, hard.

And I was still stuck. With him.

I shivered as that sliver of fear unfurled into something else.

18

MICAH

"Want to grab a couple beers from the fridge?" I said in the lightest voice I could muster. Not easy when I wanted to growl.

She made her careful way to the kitchen, reminding me that she must still be sore as hell and in no way up for the kind of long, hard session that was flashing through my mind right now. Of course, it'd been so many years since I'd done it that I was pretty sure I wasn't up for that either. I'd probably last about five seconds. Already, my cock was throbbing angrily at me, demanding that I do something about this situation.

Using the bottom of her shirt—*my* shirt—to protect her hand, she unscrewed the caps before throwing them in the trash. Something about that clogged my throat. Jesus, she was delicate. Her skin was soft, bruised to hell now, and totally breakable. If the fluted edge of a screw top was too much for her, what the hell was I? She needed tender and careful, not coarse and blunt. *Animalistic*, she'd called it.

Knowing it didn't stop the images from coming. Getting *in* her, seated deep and tight. Watching her face while I pounded…

"You want this here?"

Oh. My beer.

I lifted my chin toward the table. Couldn't walk away from the counter sporting this hard-on. I'd have to let her eat on her own at this rate. Or carry the chicken real low on my way over there.

I finished carving, piled the dog bowls high with chunks of thigh meat—their favorite—grabbed the baked potatoes from the oven, and buttered the green beans. She came to get the sides, making all kinds of comments about them, when really, it wasn't anything special. I ate this kinda stuff all the time.

Well, maybe not two roast chickens at a time, but I made all my food. What else was I supposed to do with my time? No TV, no violent-ass video games, no girlfriend. Just the dogs, the job, and this.

Me.

"This looks amazing."

I met her eye. "Taste it before you decide."

"Well, it smells good. And your stew was unbelievable. Geez, if my ex had cooked like—" She shut her eyes hard, then opened them, grabbed her beer and took a long swig, her cheeks flushing like she'd run ten miles. "I'll shut up now. Cheers."

I had to smile as she clinked her bottle to mine, met my gaze quickly and looked away again. I wished she wouldn't shut up. I liked the shit she said, from out of left field.

I'd just taken hold of the serving spoon when a strange, long-dead urge to give thanks rose up, straight from my childhood. It made sense, I guess, for it to show up here and now, after all these years of devoutly avoiding anything resembling religion. I tried to ignore it, but something about the situation, the day, the fact that she was here, made it impossible.

"You, um, you say grace or anything?" I served her a potato and some beans, pointed to a thigh and nodded my thanks when she put it on my plate.

"Not usually. You?"

"Thinking we should."

"Oh. Yeah. You're right. It's Christmas Eve. I should have thought of it." She put her hands out and I took them, did my best not to notice the details of short, soft fingers, weaving through mine.

She watched me solemnly, tightened her hands, and gave me the courage to say the words I'd never once uttered in my life. "I want to give thanks for this food, for the heat and the, uh," I shot her a look, "company."

Her smile was small, decorous, as if we were being watched by God.

I squeezed her hands, ready to let them go.

"Wait. I want to thank you, Micah, um…"

I swallowed, waiting for her to finish, then realized she'd forgotten my last name. "Graham."

"Micah Graham. Thank you for everything you've done. The meals, the bed, the…" she glanced at my bedroom door behind me, then back. "Thank you for living here. For being home to save me. For hearing the crash, for running down and pulling me out. For being so strong." Her eyes were shiny now and I needed her to stop. I couldn't handle tears from this woman.

I tried to release my hand, to reach out and make her quit it, but she wouldn't let go.

"Listen. *Please.* Thank you for being a man who needs his solitude enough to live here. Right here, where I needed you." She leaned forward, brought our hands to her mouth, in something like a prayer, and whispered one last *thanks* against my skin, before letting me go.

I wasn't sure what I was supposed to say to that—certainly not *Amen* or *You're Welcome*—so I stayed silent, digging into my food with significantly less appetite than I'd had a few minutes ago.

19

CHRISTA

I felt hollowed out inside. Exhaustion probably wasn't helping. And the other stuff. The way this man's presence plucked at my nerves, the way he turned my body on, set on this constant low hum.

And now I'd gone and embarrassed him. So, that was good.

I sniffed and looked around, in search of distraction.

Food. That would work. I took a bite and sighed. "This is delicious."

Micah grunted, not quite meeting my eyes.

What a contradiction this guy was, with his wild exterior, when so much about him, from this meal, to his house, and the way he'd treated me so far spoke of absolute civility. Somebody'd taught him right.

"Did you say you had four sisters?"

He huffed, set down his silverware, and took a

swig of his beer. "Yeah."

"Older? Younger? Where do you fall in there?"

"I'm the youngest."

"Holy crap. What was that like?"

"Good." He shrugged. "Arguments, screaming. A lot of laughing. And advice. So much advice."

"About what?"

"Everything. Girls, friends, school, what I should wear." He smiled now, for real, and his handsomeness hit me like a punch to the gut.

"What was Christmas like with that many kids?"

"Insane."

"How?"

"Somebody was always pissed off about a present not being good enough or not what they wanted." He grinned and his shoulders lifted. "My dad used to measure the boxes. If the girls didn't get the exact same number and size, every year, they'd lose their minds."

"Geez. That sounds stressful." But also very, very fun.

"What about you?"

"I was kind of spoiled, I guess." Oh, crap. I would *not* tear up again. I refused. "Just me and Dad and my grandparents."

He frowned. "No mom?"

"Dad had custody. She wasn't in the picture."

We ate silently for a while. I kept picturing

little Micah, surrounded by screaming girls.

"What you smiling at?"

"Oh." I *was* smiling. Funny I hadn't noticed. "I always wanted sisters."

He let out another little huff of amusement. "Wasn't all a walk in the park. When I was real little, they dressed me up in their clothes. Makeup and everything. Took me out into the neighborhood to show me off."

I almost spat out my beer.

"You like that, huh?"

"Can't picture it."

"Wasn't always this hairy." He rubbed his beard one-handed, then sobered. "Dad wasn't into it. Shut it right down."

"Don't suppose you have any pictures of those days?"

"No." He threw me a dirty look and finished his beer. "Want another?"

"Sure."

He went and pulled out the entire six-pack, grabbed a couple, which he opened and put on the table, then put the other two out on the front porch.

"Shouldn't open the fridge too much."

"Oh, right." I eyed him as he sat back down at the table. "You have a lot of experience with outages up here?"

"Every year."

"You like it." It wasn't a question. I could see that it satisfied him, in some way, to be alone in the wild, without power, no connection to the outside world. How would that be, not to have to worry about anything but survival? "I get that. Must feel good to be cut off for a while."

"Yeah?" His look was skeptical. "You'd want a shower eventually." *City girl.* He didn't have to say the words for me to hear them tacked onto the end of that sentence.

"Probably. But I don't mind the occasional dirty weekend." I was talking about a day or two spent in PJs, not leaving the house or showering, but the way his expression changed told me he was seeing something different. "That's not what I meant."

"What?" His voice was low, almost a whisper, his eyes heavy lidded, but sparkling with what looked a whole lot like interest, his tone almost teasing.

"Your mind's on an entirely different kind of dirty." I could easily have pretended I didn't know what he meant, ignored the way he watched me, the shift in the air.

"One of those weekends where people stay in and watch movies in their nighties? Eat ice cream and shit?"

"Not quite." I don't think he even noticed that he'd leaned over the table toward me. "I'm picturing you up here, alone, doing some kind of outdoorsy stuff." I waved vaguely toward the front door. "No music or movies or internet. Just pure, unadulterated survival."

"Keeps me sane."

I imagined me—us—in this cabin, the way we were today, except in bed, together. I wouldn't need too much distraction if I had this guy around. From out of the blue, something occurred to me. "You have a girlfriend?"

"No."

"Why not?"

"Other than my sisters and clients, you're the first woman I've spoken more than ten words to in ages."

My brows flew up in surprise. "Why?"

He shrugged. "Don't know. Haven't been interested."

My pulse quickened. Could I throw aside my insecurities and ask him? "Are you now? Interested?" There was a slight tremble to my voice.

Looking shell-shocked, he sat back in his chair, his Adam's apple bobbing once.

Oh, crap. There I went again, voicing thoughts better left in my head. "Never mind. Forget I asked. It's the kiss thing, you know. I thought maybe—"

"I'm interested."

I opened my mouth to respond, and closed it.

We watched each other, the last of our food forgotten, fire crackling cozily in the wood stove, the dogs snoring lightly from the hearthrug. Outside, the wind whistled through the trees.

"You?" He hadn't moved, but the energy

around him changed, grew expectant, tense.

"Yeah," I whispered.

"Is it 'cause I saved you?"

"Partly." I couldn't lie now that I'd opened up once. How the hell could I parse out this insane attraction? I'd spent less than 24 hours with the guy, so yeah, the fact that he'd saved my life probably had something to do with wanting to jump his bones. But not everything. This wasn't a savior thing. It went deeper than that. "You're also ridiculously hot." He opened his mouth and I went on. "You're kind, generous, interesting. You give the best massage I've ever had—including professionals—and you can cook." I took in the dogs with a lift of the chin. "I'm clearly not the only female around here who thinks highly of you."

"I'm a moody bastard."

"Haven't seen that yet."

"I fly off the handle."

"As long as it's not at me."

"Never." His lips tightened and his eyes glittered with a small taste of that vengeful rage he'd shown this morning. "I reserve that for nutsacks who force themselves onto women."

This man. Good God, this man. "I could like you. I could really, really like you."

"Not much for relationships."

Half-nervous, half-excited, I opened my mouth and asked, "How are you for dirty weekends?"

"Everybody's got skeletons, right?"

"What do you want with mine?"

"Maybe I want you to be human, instead of this ideal male of the species."

I snorted. "Hilarious."

"No, really. There's like nothing wrong with you. You're a total catch."

"So, you need me to tell you about my asshole days?" She wanted asshole? I'd give her asshole. "I used to go out, on leave, and screw three, four women in one night. Bar bathrooms that smelled like piss. Dark, filthy alleys, cars. Wherever. How's that for respecting women?"

"They wanted it?"

"Yeah."

"Then what's the problem?"

"Problem is that I never made any connections. Never fell in love, never gave a shit. Guys around me tied the knot, had kids, dug roots, and I just kept being an asshole."

"You regret it now?"

This wasn't the conversation I thought we'd be having and, suddenly, I was annoyed at her for trying to scratch the surface or get under my skin or whatever it was she was up to. "Hell if I know."

"Who was here for you when you came home?"

"I was on my own."

"Your sisters?"

"They've all got too much going on." Every

one of them, along with my parents, had tried to get me to move in with them, but I couldn't stand the idea of being dead weight. "Last thing any of them need is one more person to take care of."

Slowly, she nodded, her gaze steady on me as she set her glass on the table. When she came back, she got close, one knee bent between us, leaned forward and bypassed my mouth to whisper into my ear. "I think I've found your weakness."

"Yeah?"

"Yep." She inhaled against me and let out the breath on a low, happy note. "You don't let anyone take care of you the way you take care of them. I'll bet your muscles hurt, too, from carrying me up here? Would you let me massage you right now?"

They did. Every part of me felt used up. But I felt that way most days. Because pushing myself to the limit was my M.O. Aches were the norm.

"Don't need a massage."

"How about a thank you? For saving my life?"

In a flash, I saw her on her knees, her mouth on my cock, my hands wound tightly in that short, dark hair. It was…wrong.

"Don't need your thanks."

"What do you need, then, Micah? What do you truly want, deep down in that part of you that never gets taken care of?"

Another flash—this one to my bed: morning

sex, the lazy, slow kind I'd always imagined people having before waking fully. *I want that.*

"You don't need to—"

"No. No, you just thought of something. Something you're into. What is it?"

"Look." I pulled away, but she followed me, up and onto my lap and, suddenly, this wasn't funny anymore. She was messing with my fantasies, *becoming* them in a way I didn't know how to handle. "I don't want anything, okay?"

"Oh. Right. I pushed too hard." Her weight shifted, as she moved to get off, looking crushed, like I'd killed her kitten or stolen her backpack or some shit. "I do that sometimes. I'm sorry."

I put a hand on her thigh to hold her still, let her feel how worked up she'd already made me and, when she didn't make another effort to pull away, wrapped my hand around her neck and dragged her mouth to mine.

This kiss was different from before. This one held the promise of what lay ahead. Fewer questions, less hesitation. We'd cleared one thing up. We both wanted this. Or some semblance of it. I liked the way she kissed, humming a little, twisting in my lap, letting me take the lead and then nipping at me when she wanted it back. I liked the way she smelled, up close. Not flowery than some of those women I remembered from way back when. Fresh, clean. Like soap. Made sense, I guess, since she didn't have any perfume or lotions or whatever with her.

Her tongue, when it hit mine, was soft and sleek, and it made me wonder what her pussy would feel like, how it would taste. Fuck, it'd been years since I'd gotten my mouth on a salty-sweet woman. Now that I had, I wanted to taste every part of her.

21

CHRISTA

*T*here are rules to dating, to making the first move, the next, taking it further, upping the ante. It's always felt kind of choreographed, to me. He moves in for the first kiss, or I do, if he's hesitant. We start with lips—except for that one guy, who swooped right in with what I'll always think of as his tongue erection—introduce tongues, slowly put our hands on each other's bodies. This is if it goes right, of course. I've had other experiences, too, like most women I know. Unwanted hands, kisses, words, pics. Case in point: asshole boss who palmed my breast before I decked him.

With Micah, it wasn't so much a fast-forward as an explosion of everything at once. I couldn't say whose tongue moved first or who grabbed hold of the other's hair. No knowing if I bit him or he bit me, or who started the crazy grind at our crotches.

He shifted, arms around me, until I was beneath him on the sofa, covered me with that great big body, and showed me just how wild it could get between us. His breath was as shuddery and frantic as mine, his mouth all over me. He drew a long, hot trail from my lips to my jaw, under it to that sweet, sensitive spot on my neck, where he set my nerves off and turned me into a writhing, moaning shadow of a human being.

And all the while, I felt him between my legs, his erection through his work pants and my long underwear, a constant tease. I wanted to touch it. If only he'd let me reach down there, I'd get my hands on it, measure it, feel the heat of him there.

But every time I tried, he'd knock me away, trail his lips lower, open up some new brand of torture I had no idea existed.

Another try, another foiled attempt, except this time, he kept his hand on my wrist, held me, loosely, but irrefutably.

"Don't reach down again." His voice was low, almost angry.

"I want to touch you."

"You'll touch me when I'm ready."

Oh, shit. Bossy, huh? Did I like bossy?

"When will that be?" I was breathing hard, the words shakier than I'd intended. Bossy, it seemed, was just the thing.

He settled back on his haunches, somehow keeping his weight off me, leaned over, and tapped the armrest beneath my head. "Reach back here. Hold on and don't let go."

Yeah. Be bossy. Tell me what to do. Tell me how to do it.

My pulse went so wild it narrowed my vision. "Or what?"

Already dark in the half-light from the fire, his eyes searched my face, before traveling down my body. "You like this, Christa? Me giving orders?" His gaze was hard on mine now, curious, and sharp as diamonds.

"Yes." The word came out embarrassingly hoarse. Less than a whisper.

"You want me to stop, or you like something different, just say so. No safe word, no pretending or bullshit. Just plain English. You want it, you ask and it's yours. Got it?"

Heart thumping a million beats per minute, I stared at him, the moment suddenly overshadowed by flashbacks of dates gone bad. Men who'd wanted porn scenarios instead of reality. I'd been truly frightened with a couple of those guys.

I concentrated hard on him. If ever there was a time to be scared, this was it, wasn't it? Absolutely alone at this enormous man's mercy, I should feel fear.

"You need to stop?"

I shook my head.

His brows lowered and, for the first time since we started making out, there was a hint of indecision there. "Then tell me. Tell me you like the way I'm…being."

I looked at Micah, who'd saved me, taken care of me, and now wanted me to tell him exactly what I wanted in words.

The answer was crystal clear. I'd trust this man with my life. And he was offering the stuff my fantasies were made of.

"Don't stop, Micah. I like it."

"You sure? 'Cause this is working for me, but honestly, anything would work, and I don't want you to feel like you have to. For any reason."

I nodded, embarrassingly eager to move on with this, to see where he'd take it. How far. "Yes, yes. A lot." I couldn't help a hint of whininess. "Come *on*."

He straightened with a self-satisfied compression of the lips.

"All right."

The look he gave me now was subtly different. Meaner, more remote. No longer the guy who'd blushed at dinner, but the stranger I'd known since last night. The kind of guy who pulled women from falling cars one day and fucked them senseless the next.

Our dirty weekend had officially begun.

Slower than before, he looked me up and down, made a show of it, arrogant as hell. We were doing what he wanted, his grim smile told me, on his time. It was the hottest thing I'd ever seen, the hottest I'd ever felt.

"Use one hand to pull up your shirt. *My* shirt." His words lit me up like a Christmas tree. *Show me your tits,* I wanted him to say. *Make it crasser, filthier. Take advantage of me. Make me feel dirty.*

Oh, wow. Who the hell was I? Could I be the strong woman who kneed her asshole boss in the crotch and still want to be this man's…object?

My eager hand didn't give me time to think about it. It reached down, grabbed ahold of the fabric of this man's shirt, suddenly the sexiest thing I'd ever felt against my skin, and yanked it up.

His eyes gleamed, fierce and hungry. I could have sworn I felt them on my skin, touching, weighing, heating me as they went.

"Nice."

Oh, crap, that one word, so freaking innocuous in everyday conversation, so banal, so absolutely useless, was like a jolt of electricity to my weirdo wick.

"Big, soft. Overflowing."

Why? Why did him talking about my breasts as if they were something on display in a shop window, instead one of my most tender, sensitive parts, turn my insides to molten lava? My hips strained up, needing pressure.

"Stop that."

I froze, as if caught, trapped, terrified, and blinked. My eyes were huge on him, sucking him in like oxygen, willing to take just this if he wouldn't let me touch.

I drank him in, from the shorn, dark hair clinging to his skull, over his wide forehead, thick straight brows, low above those deep-sunk eyes. They'd been light today, blue, I was pretty sure, but now they were all pupil, daring me to dive in. A devil luring me into the depths. And, for a few strange seconds, more than his touch or the sight of his body, I wanted to explore that brain of his, to visit his dark places, learn them, wallow in them, maybe brighten them.

With a start, I emerged from whatever strange limbo I'd gone to. What the hell, man?

I ignored the question on his face and lifted my hips again and, when he pulled away, stroked him with my gaze from those wide, squared-off shoulders, over the tuft of dark hair at the collar of his work shirt, to the obvious outline of his cock below.

"Good. I like it when you look at me like that. Look your fill." I made as if to touch him and he reared back. "But you don't touch. You don't put your hands on me. I'm the one who touches this body. I'm the one who decides. You still good with that?"

I nodded.

He put one rough palm to my breast and I groaned.

22

MICAH

*H*ad it always been like this with women and I'd just forgotten? Had time just worn down all this bright, frantic need to something dull and kinda fun? Satisfying, like taking a leak.

Nothing like this. This was more than fun. It wasn't, actually, fun at all.

Jesus, no wonder I didn't do this anymore. I was out of control, wild, willing and able to do just about anything to get myself into this woman, under her skin. To get her to moan like that again —like we weren't two people having a conversation with our bodies, but sharing something deeper, wilder, more elemental. Connection.

It scared the shit out of me.

She said my name, the two syllables like music on her lips, and I couldn't stop. Her tits were everything I looked for—soft and heavy, filling my hands like water from a fountain, like the tenderest, most elemental part of a person. When my calluses made feeling impossible, I ran the backs of my knuckles along their plump, satiny sides.

I'd planned to take my time, but that feeling—the ultimate bliss of that curve—shoved everything into overdrive. I bent, put my face between her breasts, and breathed her in…

"Fuck, you smell good." Another sucking inhale, full of her—my new oxygen—and I turned, grasped her breast and pulled, putting her nipple right where I needed it.

Oh, shit, she was a dream. It was hard and red and big as a cherry and it was all I could do to kiss her before scraping her with my teeth. She gasped and writhed beneath me and, still hunched like some fucking maniac, I knocked her knees aside with one of mine, put that pouty little point into my mouth, leaned back to watch her face, and sucked.

"No no no no no no."

I stilled, dropped her nipple. "No?"

"Yes. Yes, I mean yes! God, don't stop, Micah. Don't."

A weird savagery worked its way from my cock to fill my chest, then back down again, pumping more blood into me, making me rock hard and ready. "You're screaming no, like you don't want this, but then you say you do. Which is it?"

"Huh?" Her eyes were fuzzy, her face and neck and chest bright red, like I'd slapped her. "I want it."

Gaze steady on hers, I leaned to the side for her other breast, ran my beard over her nipple, and watched the tiny changes in her face. A widening of those prim, wet little lips into a perfect *oh*, a fluttering of her dark lashes, an almost inaudible shudder. The connection between us sizzling, I reached out my tongue and licked, just the tip of that ripe little fruit, circled it once and then sank onto it, wishing I could consume every bit of her whole. "I want to fuck you." With a finger, I drew a gentle line along her breastbone. "Right here."

Her chest rose and fell, sudden as a convulsion.

"But first, I'd better taste the rest of you." Letting this rough desire lead, I licked a path over the giving flesh of her belly, to where my pants rode low on her plush hips. "You smell amazing."

She blinked, appeared to wake up, maybe, shifted minutely, like she'd push me off her.

"No. Don't move." I pressed my weight back, moved lower, let my breath heat her pussy, through black long underwear that had no right to be this fucking sexy. "I want to smell you, you let me do it." I put my mouth to her, open, hungry. "I want to eat you, you fucking let me."

She huffed out a low, inhuman-sounding groan and squirmed.

"Stop moving and pull these down."

"You want me to—"

"Don't question it, Christa. Just pull down the pants and show me your pussy."

She gasped, bit her lip, and shivered. Jesus, I liked this game. The harder I made my voice, the more glazed her eyes got.

I gave her room, watched her tug at the waistband, bringing it down, past her ass and thighs, where I took over.

Goosebumps covered her body, from neck to thighs.

"You warm?"

She nodded, slow and kind of out of it.

Out of breath, weak in places and hard as fuck in others, I separated her legs, and kneeled between them.

"You're beautiful." Flushed, clearly aroused, smelling of wet, welcoming woman, she was everything I hadn't let myself dream of in years. "Look at this pussy, all shiny and juicy. All pink and open, like it wants my cock.

She made a little denial sound in her throat. Instead of ignoring it, I followed a weird instinct and stretched up over her again. With my weight on one arm, I bent close, wrapped my hand loosely around her neck, and kissed her cheek. "Like you were made for me. Straight out of my fantasies."

She swallowed under my hand, turned and

met my eyes, hers big and glassy and dark as a summer night sky.

"I could worship this body for hours. Days. You gonna let me do that?"

She nodded, the movement slight, but there.

"Good." I tilted my head enough to kiss her, deep and wet. Owning her while she owned me. "Now, open your legs for me and let me look at that beautiful pussy."

23

CHRISTA

*Y*eah, this wasn't how I'd pictured this at all. Not when I'd felt that first inkling of desire, or admired his body, or even when we'd talked about a dirty weekend. I'd pictured him efficient and quick, the way he'd stacked wood and cooked dinner. Not slow and intense. Definitely bossy, but not so...*into* me, I guess.

Silly, right?

Maybe not, though, because I wasn't typically that into guys, either. I expected sexual excitement, the thrill of newness, definitely. I'd even fantasized about encounters—usually anonymous, the man a faceless taker—where I'd been completely turned on. Utterly sexual, an object of desire.

What I hadn't imagined, even in those private moments, was that a man could turn me into something more sensual than human. And it wasn't just the place between my legs talking, it was every part of me—my brain, my skin, down to my most basic parts—atoms, molecules. Somehow, the way he touched me, talked to me, even looked at me, reduced me to a big, beating pulse. Quickening when my brain got involved, then lulled into a syrupy slow rhythm.

All I could think, while he stroked one sandpaper hand down my side was, *I must be drunk.*

Well, Jesus, if that's what it is then don't let me sober up.

Ever.

He returned to kneeling between my legs, saying words I couldn't understand, hunkered down and put his mouth to me.

Oh, holy night.

Lips, kissing, so gently, I almost thought I'd imagined it. Another long, languorous kiss made me moan and reach for his head. His hair was too short to grab onto, so I scrabbled lower for purchase, latched onto his beard.

He growled and deepened the kiss, brought some tongue to the job, turned my insides to mush, then lower, forcing me to release my hold on him. His nose glided between my lips, down then back up to press to my clit and—

Ooooooooooh, you're kidding me.

How had I not known a man could do that with his nose? Another swipe up and it was his beard rubbing me. Good God, did the man have no taboos, no limits? He used every tool, everything he had to make me feel good.

Another slick slide and his mouth was back, thirsty for me, consuming me like a man starved and my pussy was going to save him. I almost laughed at the way I was thinking about this guy. Until he circled my clit with his tongue, then nibbled it.

"Oh, God. Oh, God." And then, because he wanted me to use his name, I let it go. A song. A prayer to this. "Micah."

"Yeah." The word rumbled against my flesh, dark and needy. "You taste amazing. Heaven. I want to eat you all night. All fucking weekend."

Impossibly, my nipples got harder at that thought. Like he'd make me come and come and keep going. I'd never get him to stop. Jesus, he could kill me with this tongue. This raw, aching hunger.

His hands slid under my ass and around my thighs to open me wider, to look at me before putting his face back to me like he'd been hungering for this—for me—for ages.

Another lick, another swipe, faster this time, his attention tight on my clit, where I concentrated every bit of my focus, too.

When his finger entered me, I wasn't ready. At all.

I made a high, startled sound and he stilled. "This okay?"

"Yeah." I giggled, full of nerves and

excitement and the unexpectedness of this entire encounter. "Yeah, sorry. Surprised me."

"Good surprise or bad?"

"Good," I breathed. "Definitely good."

He pressed the finger in deeper and I went still.

"This looks amazing. My finger in your tiny pussy. You're so pink here, like a flower. Can't imagine how you'll take my cock." I tightened convulsively around his finger and he went still. "You like it? When I say shit like that?"

All I could do was nod.

"When I talk about how it's gonna feel when I wedge myself into you—fuck, can I even fit?" His finger slid out and my hips shifted up as if to hold him in. "Better get you ready, right? Or maybe we won't fuck." He paused. "That's all right, too. If you don't want to. But I'll think about it. I'll spend weeks, years, fantasizing how it would feel to have you stretched out around me." After a beat of silence, he said, "You want to watch this?"

Oh. That hadn't even occurred to me. Now that he'd proposed it, I needed to see the place where we connected.

"Grab that." He reached back and threw me a cushion, which I jammed behind my head. Once he was in place and I was settled, he met my eyes, bent, brow creased with concentration, and with his mouth on me, lifted his gaze to mine again. His stare pinned my upper body in place as surely as his thick arms restrained the rest of me.

The sensations were different with him watching me. Sharper, as piercing as his eyes. Ensnared in that look, each stroke, each lick, each wet kiss cut deeper. Past layers of embarrassment, self-consciousness, and awkward humor, he went straight to that place again—it was wild and open and wanting.

I craved him in me, deep and hard—invading, like the Viking he resembled. I wanted this shared look, but closer. So close I wouldn't have to see his eyes.

And then it was back, his finger, sliding in, another joining it, pulling me roughly apart. I let out a sound, shut my eyes, and escaped. He didn't thrust, the way guys had before, but stroked me inside, tenderly, slowly, inexorably. He knew what he was doing and he took his time.

Why rush? I pictured him saying. This man who'd chosen to live on nature's timeline, instead of in the mad rush preferred by modern man.

A deep thrust, a twist, another finger pushed inside, almost painful in that way that felt so good.

I groaned, desperate for that other thing, imagining this wasn't his finger, but that erection I'd felt against me.

He deepened the penetration, quickened the pace on my clit, reached up with his other hand, skimmed my belly, kneaded it once, and went higher to twist my nipple—hard.

I came, my body unexpectedly seizing, tightening around his fingers, bumping his face.

My hand appeared from out of nowhere and squeezed his as if to share some of this unbearably twisted tension.

He didn't move, just waited, watching. And, oh, those eyes sent my body up again—insides fluttering on something that was as raw and uncomfortable as embarrassment. Or shame.

I reddened a bit more and bit down on the sounds I wanted to make, the truth suddenly obvious: I'd just been more unabashedly, openly sexual with this man than I'd ever been in my life. I'd shown him more of my raw, aching innards than anyone else had seen.

And I'd known him for just one day.

24

MICAH

*T*hings fractured when she came, reason took off in one direction and that wild thing hunkered low and deep in my belly took over.

Mine, it said, pushing me up the sofa, knees planted between hers, stiff arms framing her chest, while I bent to take her mouth.

Mine, it whispered as I yanked off my shirt, then reached down to unbutton and unzip myself, shoving down my shorts to release the pressure and get just a feel of her against me.

Mine, it screamed when her hand grasped my throbbing cock and gave it a tentative stroke, then another, bolder one. I met her third one with a thrust of my hips.

When she lifted her hips and slid it against that soft, welcoming place I now knew like the back of my hand, it would have been so easy to slide inside. Her wetness coated me, marking my dick as surely as she'd marked my face.

Claiming me.

The way I wanted to claim her. *Own* her.

Another tilt of the hips and I could do it, lodge myself inside. It wouldn't be my fault any more than hers. We'd get carried away, break some rules. Who could blame us, when shit had gotten so hot so fast? Who could blame me when she looked like the pure, wild sex of my fantasies?

Her hand reached into my pants, ran around the side and tightened on my ass, pushing me closer.

"Fuck. Don't do this to me, Christa."

Her hips rose and fell, then made a long slow circle, grinding us together hard.

"Do what?"

"Push me too far. Make me lose it."

Another teasing press and a low sound, from deep in her throat. Like a laugh, only darker. I glanced at her face.

"You're gonna make me come."

"I want you to come." She lifted her torso to rub her tits to my chest, the sound of nipples rasping through hair loud in this quiet room.

"On your pussy."

"Okay." Her eyes widened and she gave a little nod, setting something off inside me.

I thrust against her half a dozen times before her hand tightened. "Hang on."

"Yeah?"

"Can you sit? On the edge, here?"

Breathing ragged, I nodded, maneuvered a little awkwardly, with my waistband around my thighs, and got to a place where I could pull my pants down farther and sit. She slid to her knees on the floor and my mouth dropped open.

"*Fuck me.*"

"Let me suck you first."

I didn't bother correcting her. It didn't matter if she thought I'd meant it as an order. All that mattered was that she leaned in and kissed the crown of my dick, the way I'd kissed her pussy before. Like it was my mouth. My vision went kaleidoscopic. Jagged pieces scattered around the room—flame from the candles, the glint of her hair, her eyes, and that mouth.

"Yeah. Oh, fuck, yeah. Suck me hard."

As if my words set a match to her fuse, she put her mouth around me, tightened, and did what I asked.

"Holy mother of God." First saying grace, now praying. This woman brought religion right back into my life. "Harder."

I was dying to sink my hands into her hair, to hold her tight, maybe drag her closer. Instead, needing some kind of control, I set them on my knees, and held on.

Down and up, once, twice, so deep I felt the back of her throat. My fingers flexed of their own volition.

Tighter, her mouth worked me, one of her

slender hands fisting the root of my cock. Her eyes met mine.

"I'm close."

She looked to the side and focused on my twitching hand as she suckled the tip of my erection. "Do it."

I gave her a dark look, pretended not to understand.

"Put your hand in my hair." Her voice was raspy, her breath hot on my dick. "I like it when you're pushy." Her teeth raked a hot trail down one side, then up the next, followed by her tongue. She stayed there, licking my balls, suckling slowly like we had all night. Which we didn't.

"I'll come if you keep doing that." She didn't stop, so I threaded my fingers into her hair, tightened them, and showed her how to make it happen.

I couldn't understand what she said next, with my cock down her throat. But when I loosened my hand and gave her a chance to talk, she threw an angry look my way and impaled herself, again. Again. Christ, again.

Somehow, my other hand joined the first, cradled her head, not tightly, but steadily, and showed her how fast I wanted it, how hard.

"Suck it. Hard. Yeah, like that."

She moaned, the sensation so low and subtle, it felt like it came from me.

"I want to come in your mouth." Her eyes met mine, gave me a slow blink. "You want that? Or on your tits." Anywhere on her. In her.

She shimmied and backed off, leaving me alone and worried I'd offended her for a few frantic seconds. But then she nudged me, urging me to scoot back to where she'd been not so long ago, and climbed up and over me. It took a while for my lust-fogged brain to realize what she was doing with her hands on her breasts and her chin down.

But when I did... Goddamn. This was it. Dream woman in my house.

"I'm gonna come fast like this."

This couldn't be real. This person who read my mind, pulled out the best parts, and dropped them at my feet like Brownie dropping a stick.

"Do it." She put my cock between her breasts, grabbed my hand so I'd squeeze them together, and slid her body up and down. Her mouth, at the top, sucked the tip of my dick—a warm surprise.

I couldn't catch my breath when I came, and only just managed to warn her with a guttural yell, before biting down hard and gritting my teeth as lightning blew through me.

In tight, deafening shock, I watched come shoot from my cock, lashing her in long, white stripes, before she engulfed me in that mouth, sucking the last drops of pleasure and owning me.

Half-dead, emptied of everything but the barest spark of intelligence, I somehow managed to pull her over me before collapsing onto the sofa.

25

CHRISTA

*T*here was good sex and then there was obliteration, black hole, no-Christa-left-inside-this-empty-shell, just a shuddering, barely conscious body sex.

Yeah, that was me, plastered on top of this big man, who didn't seem to mind my weight or the stickiness between us. He sighed and tightened his arms around me.

I should get up. Instead, I rubbed my face into his chest, sucked in a wood smoke-and Micah-laced breath, and just…stayed.

Probably ten minutes passed as our bodies cooled, him caressing my back slowly with one large hand. Finally, I shivered hard enough that he stopped the stroking and urged me up.

"How about a bath?"

The dogs' heads rose simultaneously, as if lifted by the same puppet master—Brownie open-mouthed and eager and Bear a little dastardly with that single standing ear.

"I thought there wasn't any water."

"No. But I'll get the generator running and we'll have hot water in no time."

"Oh, uh, sure."

Still wrapped in the blanket from the bed, I watched him stomp into boots and slam outside, with the dogs shooting out ahead of him, barking as if it were playtime, instead of late at night.

Guess I wasn't the only one who had to pee.

I got up, took a candle to the bathroom and returned to the sofa to wait cocooned in the soft blanket. It seemed pointless to put clothes back on before bathing.

Let's take a bath.

Did he mean together?

The sudden, overly loud sound of an engine outside had me close to jumping out of my skin.

Immediately, as usual, my brain supplied the worst-case scenario: it must be Jonathan, my boss. Who else was close enough to drive here?

No, dummy, it's the generator.

I let out a relieved breath, listening to the hum of the refrigerator kicking in.

And, even if it were Jonathan, I wasn't scared of that jerk.

But—I hugged my legs to my body and dropped my head to my knees—I was still out a job. Shit.

Shit. Shit. Shit.

In search of a distraction, I stood, blanket wrapped tightly around me, and took a quick turn around the room.

There wasn't much. A lot of windows for such a small place. Clean, solid furniture, with absolutely no distractions like junk or knickknacks. Sparse.

Something glinted in the corner by the front door. A shopping bag. I moved closer. It was filled with gifts wrapped in holiday paper. I squatted and looked at the card on the top gift. To Micah. The one beside it also had his name on it. One of the cards didn't have an envelope. I shouldn't read it. I wouldn't.

It was open, though, and the letters were big and, clearly written by a kid.

"Dear Micah. Miss you. Sorry you will not be at Christmas. Love, Vic."

I straightened, stepped guiltily from the bag and bumped into the desk behind me. I just caught a tottering lamp before it fell.

Coasting on that little spike of adrenaline, I picked up a black-framed photo I'd knocked face down. Wow. That was a big family. Was he in there? I squinted, but didn't see him. Huh.

Beside the photo was a fanned out pile of business cards. I'd probably messed those up with my butt. I straightened them and, after a moment's hesitation, picked one up.

It was plain white, with black lettering—Arial font—and listed his name and number: MICAH

GRAHAM, Certified Arborist. I turned it over in search of a website or email. Nothing.

I considered pocketing one, but then remembered I didn't have a purse or even a pocket to put it in at this point. I returned it to the pile and neatened it up, with a strangely final feeling.

Not much for relationships, he'd said.

Fine. A dirty Christmas. That was it. No strings, no cards, no numbers.

Although I'd definitely look up exactly what it was arborists did. Okay, I'd obsess over it. Probably google him, too, if I was honest.

But, man, how did he even run a business nowadays without a website? I swiveled around. Or even a computer, as far as I could tell.

Course, he might have an office in town. But then he'd have put that address on his cards, wouldn't he?

Did he get enough work like this to survive? The man was so self-sufficient, I couldn't image he needed a whole lot.

That was both attractive and, suddenly, unexpectedly, heart wrenching. Despite that pile of gifts in the corner that said he had plenty of people who loved him, he'd planned to spend the holidays alone before I came along. New Year's probably wasn't even a blip on his radar.

It wasn't sad, I decided, if he didn't care. Which truly seemed to be the case.

I turned, took in the clean, cozy cabin, lit by

the candles' golden haze and the lazily snapping fire in the wood stove, and unconsciously looked for my phone.

It took me just a few seconds to remember that there'd be no Instagramming this moment. My phone was gone, along with my purse, my car. My job.

I sank onto the arm of the sofa and tried to catch my breath.

Holy shit. My life. My entire freaking life. Stupid things occurred to me—I'd kept my favorite shiny, see-though rainbow umbrella in the Jetta's trunk. My sneakers had been on the back seat. What else? What other crap did I leave in there?

No. No way was I wallowing in this…again. I needed something to do. I could clean, but there wasn't a speck of dust in the place. On a whim, I stood up, headed to the desk, grabbed a pen from the jar and a sheet of paper from the drawer, and started sketching out business card ideas.

A short while later, the door opened, startling me out of my work-focus. As I stood up, the dogs shook themselves, showering me with a fine, cold spray. My surprised yelp turned into a laugh.

"Come on, girls." Micah grabbed Bear and rubbed her down with a towel, but Brownie somehow escaped him, headed straight for me, and goosed me, her nose freezing against my thigh. I yelped and managed to grab ahold of her by the collar. My laughing attempts to drag her back to the front door were like back slapstick.

Together, we finally got them dried off. He followed them in and sat on his bench. I hesitated, hand suspended, then finally gave in to the urge to run my fingers through his hair. It was cold and wet.

"You need a rub down, too, Micah," I told him, full to bursting with this unexpected affection. I went still when I saw the look in his eye, breath caught in my throat.

"How about that bath first?" he asked, the question more threat than invitation.

26

MICAH

*G*rowing up with four siblings pretty much ensured that someone was freaking out most days. It was sometimes good, sometimes bad, often big, and always emotional. I'd never have said that I missed it, after all this time away, and these years spent alone, but holding Christa, soaking up her explosion of feelings, it occurred to me that maybe I did miss it. Maybe living alone up here wasn't all that satisfying.

It was easy, simple, quiet—all the things I'd needed after Afghanistan—but now it felt like I was excluding stuff. Stuff like this.

I turned the tap. The water was warm, but not yet hot. I filled the bath anyway, then went into the living room for the cast-iron kettle I left on the wood stove, emptied that into the bath, then set more water to boil there and in the kitchen. We'd get it hot in no time.

Christa huddled on the sofa, alternately staring at the fire, and giving me shy little smiles, and all I could think was, *Yeah. I've missed out.*

Jesus, save me from myself, I thought as I tromped back out into the snow to shut down the generator.

Christa greeted me at the door.

"Why aren't you in the bath?"

She looked confused. "Oh. I thought you and I…"

"Figured you'd want to be alone."

She started to shake her head, then compressed her lips, as if stopping herself from saying whatever was on her mind. And then, because she wasn't the sort of person who'd stop herself from being honest, she said, "I want to be with *you*."

Her eyes met mine head-on, looking defiant or stubborn, and something expanded in my chest.

In two steps, I was in front of her, dropping the blanket from her shoulders, baring her naked curves and pulling her into my cold body.

She shivered so hard that I should have pushed her away. But I couldn't. Kissing her wasn't a desire, it was a need, as real as hunger.

Had to have those lips, that tongue, her body lined up with mine, her cheeks in my palms.

I needed her closer, breasts against my chest. I needed these clothes off and—

As if she'd read my mind, her hands were at my waist, tugging at the button and zipper, then pushing my pants down. Those hands—hot and capable—tightened on my cock, pressed it down between her legs and…

"Fuuuuuck." A hot, slick slide against her didn't feel like enough. "No…condoms."

I should slow down. Stop this, since she was emotional and raw. I couldn't believe how turned on she seemed, her body shifted forward and back, like fucking, right here by the front door.

"I've got an IUD," she whispered.

"I don't have any diseases and I haven't had sex in…forever."

"Put it in me, Micah. I want you in me."

I wanted my shirt off so I could feel her nipples, wanted a bed so I could do this slowly, and patience so I wouldn't lose it before this even started, but none of that was in the cards for right now.

Because more than anything, I wanted my cock in her pussy.

I grasped her under the ass and lifted. She was right there, hot and ready, legs wrapped around my hips, and, before I could prepare for what was about to happen, she grabbed my dick, lined it up, and pushed herself down on me…

Our noises were the hottest thing I'd ever heard. They'd have told the story clear as day, without the pictures to go along.

Her grunts, low and animal, confirmed that I wasn't an easy fit. And, in all fairness, I didn't think I'd ever been this big and hard. So solid, it felt like I could hold her up against the cool door with my hard-on alone.

I bent my legs, flexed my ass, and pressed in, one slow inch at a time.

It was so good it almost hurt. I screwed my eyes shut and waited for my balls to calm down. Then down and back up, slowly and steadily nailing her to the door.

When my cock was seated deep inside, I sucked in a breath, opened my eyes…and nearly came.

Her tits hung down, heavy and so lush it hurt. Below that, her belly had that swell that I loved on a woman. And her hips, wide and soft, took me in, made me feel like home. Like this, right here, was where I should've been all these years. "Fuck me, you're beautiful, Christa."

"You keep saying that," she whispered, her voice straight out of some black and white movie.

I shifted her weight to my left arm and used my right hand to play with her tits, slowly, faking a calm I didn't think I'd ever manage around this woman. I weighed one, stroked that impossibly soft underside, then ran the back of my knuckles over her thick, round nipple. I did the same on the other side, before pinching them both. A slow stroke out of her body, then up and inside. I wanted to pound, hard and fast and so deep she'd never get me out.

Another pump, faster this time. It made her tits bounce and had her eyelids sagging shut.

"Open your eyes. Watch."

Slowly, she looked at me as I lifted her breast to my mouth, and sucked on the tip, hard. She clenched her pussy and gasped at the same time.

"Look." I pulled away, just enough to catch a glimpse of my shiny cock gliding out, then back inside—pounding myself home. *Home.* "Down."

"Oh, my God," she breathed as she stared, clearly as awed by this as I was.

"Now touch yourself. Make yourself come."

"I…I can't."

"Try."

I shifted my weight, pressed her tight to the door and gave her space to slip her right hand between our bodies. She touched herself slowly. Too slowly, if I wanted her to come before I blew. Five years without sex. Five years, but a lifetime, if I was honest, because this was like nothing I'd experienced. This woman was like no one I'd ever met.

I wanted to plant myself inside her and never come out.

"Come on, faster," I urged, feeling starved and off-kilter. Maybe insane. Definitely obsessed. "I know you need it faster to come. Do it faster."

She sent a grumpy look my way, but set to

work, rubbing herself toward orgasm, while I did my best to hold back.

"Oh, my God, Micah. Oh... Oh, my God." Her little white teeth bit into that bright red, swollen bottom lip. "I'm coming. I'm co—."

27

CHRISTA

*S*andwiched between a thick wooden door and a steel-muscled man, I orgasmed, screaming like I'd never screamed in my life. I'd never clenched so hard, never felt such a big thing inside me, never been so wide open to what was happening.

And, I don't know if it was because of my near-death experience, or the fact that this man was my own personal hero, maybe emotions or exhaustion…whatever the reason, this climax was like nothing I'd ever experienced. It hit me low and worked its way out to the tips of my limbs, my breasts, my tongue, my nose—fizzing and shimmering like I'd left the earth for a minute or two.

He stopped moving entirely, just held me through it, as if I needed to be held together. Which I probably did.

He probably also couldn't budge, with how

tightly my inner muscles held him. No way he could move a millimeter.

"I need…" I swallowed, leaned forward, looking for…

His kiss. His lips, tongue. This taste— everything I'd been missing.

He slid out, just a couple inches, then slowly pressed back in, the movement hitting all those lit- up places we'd awakened together.

"Your turn, Micah."

He shushed me, kissed me again, held me up, pressed me to the door. Taking care of me, because he couldn't be bothered to worry about himself.

"Come on. Do it." I didn't even ask myself why I wanted him to come. It wasn't something I'd considered before with a man. Did he come? Did he not? Did it matter? I mean, yes, as far as mutual satisfaction was concerned, but this was different. This was about…giving him something. Pleasure, maybe?

"I want you to come in me." Uh oh, I'd just acquired a new kink. The list, with this man, was getting long.

"Yeah?" He leaned back, eyes wide open, questioning.

"I want to feel it." And then, because I liked the way he looked at me when I said his name. "Come in me, Micah."

"Fuck." He picked up the pace, his thrusts

messier, my body a tool now, rather than the center of everything.

"Fill me with your come."

"Oh, shit." His hold under me tightened, one arm a steel band, lifting and dropping me, impaling me on his massive erection. "I've never done this before."

For a few short seconds, I thought he meant sex. Which wasn't possible.

"Never…done…what?"

"Bareback." The word, pornographic, to my ears, tightened my nipples painfully, made me clench harder around him. "Raw."

Definitely a kink. "You've never done it without protection?"

"No. No, never."

"You want to come in my pussy?"

"Oh, fuck yeah. Fuck, I want to fill you up with it."

"Yeah. Good. Do it, Micah," I urged, the devil on his shoulder. I wanted to see his face when he came, wanted to be the receptacle for all that built-up pressure. He pounded harder, pumped sloppily, grabbed my breast, twisted my nipple. He looked like chaos and pleasure and pure, feral delight. I wanted a picture of this to wank to for the rest of my life.

"Soon." Faster, almost leaving my body, concentrating hard on nothing but his cock, getting there, his arms tight and efficient. "Fuck, Oh, Fuck. Fuuuuuuuuuuuck…" The sounds coming from his mouth turned wordless, guttural and pained, his rhythm disappeared, he jerked me hard onto his body, another couple fast ones and then a final push, deep, deep inside, his teeth imprinting the side of my neck.

All of this was like a claiming—him me or me him, I wasn't sure. He pulsed inside me and I imagined I could feel his semen. I squeezed around him and he hummed.

After a few harshly drawn breaths, he dropped my legs, slumped against the door, and gave a worn half-laugh against my neck before sliding out of my body.

"That was unbelievable."

I huffed out a giggle, bereft, now that he was no longer in me, but happy. "It was."

"Yeah?"

I looked up and what I saw in that hard-planed face made my belly go squishy. "You turned me into a porn actress."

His smile was massive, his teeth big and white against that dark beard, his eyes lit up, the creases around them making him ten times more handsome. "You *were* quite the dirty talker, Christa."

"Yeah, well that's new."

"It was incredible."

I blushed and looked away. "If we're doing a dirty weekend, we might as well do it right."

"Sure." He gave me a final squeeze and

stepped back. "Let's see if we can both fit into that bath."

Since I was already naked, I started toward the bathroom. Micah's voice stopped me.

"Hang on. I'd better take off the prosthesis first."

"Oh."

I followed him through the door and he lifted his chin toward the bench built into the outside of the tub. I stayed out of his way, not sure where to go or stand, or if I should look.

When he peeled off his shirt to reveal those hard-packed muscles, scattered with hair and dark freckles, I stopped questioning things and watched, blatantly fascinated by this man's body, his face, the way he moved. The way he lived.

He yanked his pants down the rest of the way, drawing my eyes to his penis, soft now, but still attractive.

Weird. I'd never thought that before.

I blinked when he sat on the bench, and stepped out of his pants, then went to work taking off the prosthesis. He pressed what looked like a little button at the ankle, slid it off to reveal his leg, covered in layers of what appeared to be cotton tights. A black pin stuck down from the end, a few inches below his knee.

"The pin sticks into the prosthetic leg."

"Oh." I lifted my eyes to his and flushed hard, feeling caught out. "I'm sorry to stare."

"S'fine. I'd be curious, too."

"Does it hurt?"

He shook his head. "Worst pain is at night. Ghost limb pain."

"So…the pain's not real?"

"Brain thinks it's real. Feels real."

"Seems unfair."

He shrugged and focused back on his hands pulling off the black stocking thing. "Compression sock." Under it was a thicker layer, attached to the leg mechanism. "Liner." The liner looked like it was be made from thick, stretchy silicone. "To put it back on, I put on the liner, the sock, then click this into the prosthetic's socket." He ran his hand down the thick, sturdy-looking muscles of his thigh. My eyes flew up to his face, unsure. Did he want me to look at him? I took a slow step forward, hesitated, and then rested my fingers on the shiny red scar that dug a jagged trench into his thigh. The muscle here was hard, but more textured than the other side, the hair sparser in areas. When he didn't protest, I followed the thick, ridged knot of muscle and tissue over his knee—slighter than the right one—to where his leg thinned and ended a few inches below it.

He put his hand on mine, stopping the downward movement before I reached the end.

"Must be a pain, doing that every time you get up and go out or bathe or whatever."

He frowned, stroking my knuckles for a few seconds before setting my hand away. "Don't mind. Small price to pay for being alive. Walking, running. Climbing trees." He pushed up and slid into the bath, which raised the water level to an alarming degree.

"I can't fit in there."

"Sure you can." He reached forward to let some water out, then lifted his right leg and set his foot on the rim of the tub. "Plenty of room."

I'm not sure what it was about that moment— after all the hugging and massaging, the sex and orgasms, the saving of my actual freaking life— that felt different from the rest. It could have been the sight of him naked, strong and proud, or the unexpected intimacy of watching him pull off his leg, unabashed on the surface, but with a near-hidden tinge of insecurity I'd never have expected him to show. Had he opened this much of himself up to another woman?

"You getting in?"

I nodded, out of words, grabbed onto the side of the tub and sank in, with my back against his front. The heat made me shiver and sigh and helped cover up the uncomfortable knowledge that, whatever this was for him, for me, it could never be just any old encounter.

28

MICAH

*C*hrista's body fit mine like a glove. Or maybe the other way around, with me surrounding her. A fantasy come true, only so real that it hurt to hold her now, knowing that soon she'd be gone. Nothing but a short, sweet interlude in my life.

I opened my mouth to say something I'd probably regret, but she beat me to the punch.

"So, you climb trees for living?"

I huffed out a laugh and kissed the top of her head. Damn, she smelled good.

"I'm an arborist. Don't always climb trees, since a lot of my work is consulting with clients." I cupped a handful of water and poured it over her breast, watched it run down, fascinated. "Hate losing trees. And I don't tell my clients this, but getting up there with a chainsaw's my favorite part." Incapable of not touching her, I weighed her breasts in my hands, wishing I could get down and lick her there again, suck on her nipples.

"That's…you're incredible." Her chest rose and fell with heavy breaths. I did that to her. Me, nothing but a loner dude, just trying to keep my head on straight. I hadn't felt this… Power wasn't the right word, but strength wasn't it either. Whatever the word, I hadn't felt like this in ages. Years.

Maybe ever.

"You are," I whispered against the side of her head. "How the hell'd this happen, huh?"

She started to turn and I nudged her straight, not even remotely ready to show her what must show plainly on my face—this thing was bigger than a night or a weekend. Whatever the hell had brought us together—shit weather, divine providence, the fucking Holy Spirit. Whatever it was, I didn't want it to end. Couldn't let it end and feel whole anymore. "Don't."

"Don't what?"

Don't go. "Don't look at me."

She grew very still. "Why not?"

"You've torn me up inside, Christa. I'm not the same since I pulled you out of that car."

"No?"

"Mm-mm." To calm myself, or maybe just to get the attention off of me, I let one hand play with her nipple and moved the other further south, under the water, between her legs.

"How'm I supposed to go back to what I had

before?" I cleared my throat. "How do you expect me to live my…solitary life up here once you're gone?"

Her breathing was shaky, her breasts quivering. She tried to turn again and, firmer this time, I bracketed her with my arms, slid a finger inside her with my left hand, and flicked at her clit with my right. Maybe distracting her would do it. Maybe she wouldn't notice how she'd torn me apart. Or how badly I wanted to tell her about it. Like I'd spent all these years quiet—and happy that way—but suddenly, she'd unlocked some magic door and I needed to spew feelings like a damn geyser.

Like with my sisters when we were kids, the emotions here were too big to stay locked up. But I couldn't let her watch me come apart.

Another finger, sliding in to join the first, my thumb working her faster. My cock stirred to life again, which wasn't remotely surprising considering how lush her ass was, right here against me.

I pressed forward, let her feel me, and continued to drive her higher. If I did this, we could pretend she hadn't heard what I'd just said. I could pretend I didn't say it.

Her hard breathing turned to moans and my body wanted her again, which seemed impossible after so short a time. I eyed the tub, trying to figure out if we could even do it in here and then she answered the question by lifting herself up.

"Can you…can you put it in me?"

Fuck, yeah, I could do that. I reached for my cock, held it at the bottom, ran it up and down her lips a couple times to slick it with her wetness, mixed with my come from our earlier session. Like I'd marked her with it. My cock pulsed at that idea and I notched myself at her entrance, wrapped my arm around her belly and pulled her onto me.

Our movements were awkward and slow in the tub.

And, shit, she was in pain from her accident. I shouldn't push her.

"Don't move, Christa. Don't need to hurt yourself again. Just stay like that."

She stilled for a few seconds, tightened around my dick and let go, tightened and let go.

"Holy shit."

"I do my kegels."

I grinned into her shoulder, then nipped her with my teeth, and pulled her down, hard.

"Is this good?" she asked, though she had to know it was.

"Yeah. Oh, yeah."

Wet and round, sweet and smart as hell.

We fucked slow and deep for what felt like ages, concentrating on keeping the water in the bath. I'd never done anything like it before, never been so close to a person as in that moment. Like I knew her, inside and out. Like every tight contraction was a hug.

Her back to my front, her ass on my lap, my body inside her, all I could do was put my face to her shoulder and breathe.

You're my dream woman, Christa Evans. And I don't even know you.

29

CHRISTA

I'm not sure how he knew it was time, but he reached around and put his hand to my clit to rub me. Even that movement was slow, languorous, more about pleasure than the end goal.

I could almost fall asleep like this, in his arms in the warm bath. Except his finger, slow though it was, had started a spark and the orgasm couldn't be far behind.

I turned my head, caught his eyes and watched them flare hot.

"Micah." The name came out of my mouth, as syrupy and warm as everything else about this moment.

Not an explosion, but a deep thrumming that emanated outward, heating everything in its glow. I bore down on him, moaning and breathing hard and, right on the tail end of it, he thrust up with a wounded-sounding noise of his own, and joined me in this immense, intimate moment.

In the afterglow, I lay back on him, boneless, as tears slid down my face.

Shit. Shit shit shit.

I couldn't be in love with him already. I couldn't and I wouldn't, dammit.

"You okay?"

All I could do was nod, sniffling back in an attempt to hide that I was—yet again—crying.

"Bed?"

I nodded again and stood up, releasing him from my body as I did. With a slosh of water, he half rose behind me, sat on the side of the tub and snagged a towel to wrap around me. We dried off silently and quickly. After drying off completely and putting his leg back on, he gave me a couple minutes alone, saying something about heading back out to check on things.

I avoided the mirror.

His bed was cold and smelled like him and I worked hard to keep all this teary emotion inside. *Good God, woman, keep it together.*

He returned and stood silhouetted in the door for a few seconds before speaking. "I wanna come in there, but I don't want to assume."

In answer, I pulled back the covers. He sat on the bed, removed his prosthesis, and slid in beside me. His cold hands on my waist made me squeal, but when he tried pulling them away with an apology, I grabbed them and held them to me.

"It's the least I can do. You're off in the woods, turning generators on and off and I'm just lolling around your house."

"Naked." I could hear the smile in his voice as he wrapped his body around mine. Perfect spoons.

"And waiting."

"Got to tell you, Christa, this is the stuff fantasies are made of."

I wouldn't let that go to my heart. It was a dirty weekend. He didn't do relationships. Besides, though I'd let him inside my brain and my body, it wasn't like we knew each other. "Glad I can fulfill them for you."

He didn't respond. The silence dragged out.

"It's a lot of work, putting on your prosthetic leg and taking it off again, every time you get into bed or a shower or whatever."

"Don't mind. Used to it now."

"Must have been hard when it first happened."

When he didn't say anything, I figured he didn't want to talk about it. He surprised me a couple minutes later by answering. "Yeah." He sniffed. "Some guys go back, even after an amputation. I never wanted to see any of it again. Never wanted to see the inside of a barracks or a mess tent. Couldn't stand being around people, crowds, yelling. Dust and diesel and helicopters. Didn't want to smell…"

"What?"

"War."

I tried to picture what that odor would be. Did bombs have a smell? Missiles? Burning flesh? Did the scent of certain spices bring him back to a particular time in his life?

I hesitated, not wanting to pry. "Where did it happen?"

"Afghanistan."

"That's quite a change. From Afghanistan to Whatcom County."

He huffed out another almost laugh.

"And your job sounds dangerous, so it's not like you left the risk element behind."

He hummed a response.

"I saw your business cards. You don't have a website or anything on there."

"Not much for technology."

"You get enough business?"

"Get what I need."

"No desire to grow it?"

"I'd take more work, but I've got no interest in running after it."

"You probably don't want it, but...I mocked up a few new card designs for you. And put together some logo and website ideas."

"Yeah? You didn't have to—"

"I wanted to. Needed to keep busy, you know?"

He tightened his arm around my waist and I snuggled into his naked body. "What about you,

Christa? Now that you're free from your shitty boss. What are you gonna do?"

I opened my mouth to respond and shut it again.

"Don't have to answer. Just being curious."

"It's a good question. The thing is, there's what I should do and what I want to do." I thought of Granny Evans alone in her big house. "I need steady, decent income. So, I'll probably hit the employment websites as soon as…" *I get back to civilization.* I couldn't bring myself to say the words. I didn't want this to end.

"And the other thing? The dream job?"

"I'd like to help small businesses and nonprofits find their audience."

"Sounds important." He huffed against my back. "I have no idea what it means."

"So, a lot of people who open a business really love what they do. Same with a nonprofit. These are people who believe in their mission. They're not into it to hobnob with wealthy donors or market or whatever." I turned onto my back and he loosened his grip, but kept his arm on my belly.

"Makes sense."

"And most of them, especially up front, couldn't pay for a full-time PR person. If money weren't an issue, I'd start a business with different types of services. Affordable graphic design and marketing packages, general PR advice, consultation. I'd also work with nonprofits to help acquire funding and I'd only charge my fee once they got the money."

"That's…amazing."

"It's my dream job."

"Do-gooder."

I hid my smile against his chest. "I think we all know who the Good Samaritan is around here."

He let out a gruff sound and pulled me closer.

I'd never been particularly snuggly with boyfriends, but this didn't feel like an encroachment of my private space. Not even close.

I felt cocooned. Safe. *Right.*

I was in so much trouble.

30

MICAH

*I*t was too hot to sleep. Or something.

Careful not to wake Christa, I got out of bed, grabbed my crutches, and went into the other room, followed by the girls. The fire had died down, so I put a couple logs on, even though the air was suffocating.

A glance at the thermometer showed that it was 58 degrees inside. That had to be wrong. It was suffocating. I needed to go outside. Now.

I walked to the big front window and pulled back the curtain. Bright as hell out there, despite the late hour. And cold, judging from the frost on the glass.

My cabin didn't usually feel this small, or hot. This wasn't a place I escaped from, but the place I escaped *to*.

Now, she'd ruined that. Anger spiked through me, sharp as an ax.

Had to leave. I swung toward the door,

struggling to breathe and crazed enough to go outside with my crutches, buck naked, wearing a solitary slipper.

I twisted the doorknob, glanced down at my desk, and stopped.

What was that?

For no earthly reason, warning bells went off in my head. I ignored them and slid the first page toward me.

It was a series of rectangles. My business card, redesigned by someone who knew their stuff.

Even drawn out roughly in pen, her designs were good. She'd put www.micahgraham.com at the bottom and drawn climbing trees on either side. They got progressively more complicated, the pictures more detailed. The next page was just a tree, with a guy holding a chainsaw at the top. Me. On the next one, she'd added the dogs at the base of the tree. One had my silhouette leaning against a trunk, holding it up. Or maybe the tree held me up. It was sort of balanced.

The beauty of the drawings was in how simple they were—same with the business cards. They weren't all froufrou and full of useless details. When she drew, she used just enough lines to make the picture. No more than she needed. They were really good.

And, somehow, she'd captured *me* in them. Not just some random arborist, but a big, bearded loner. I looked solid in these sketches. Substantial. A part of the forest, like I belonged with those trees. Like we were born from the same stuff.

I carefully returned them to the desk and sank to the sofa and stared at the flames in the wood stove until I could breathe normally again. My body temperature dropped and the cool air seeped back in.

If I went back to bed, I could wake up with her tomorrow. Christmas Day. She might hum in her throat, back her ass up against me. I'd find her so wet I'd slide right into her, from behind. Lazy and slow in the bright, fresh morning.

Couldn't remember the last time I'd wanted something this bad—so bad it hurt. Stole my breath, suffocated me.

Actually, I could. The day I'd come to in the hospital and understood that my leg was gone. That day, I'd wanted to back up time and change the way shit had gone down. I'd begged and prayed and pleaded to God to give me another chance.

Pointless.

I rubbed my hand to my chest, hating this feeling of not enough, when I'd been fine with what I had before.

My open bedroom door called to me, made me want to get up and head in there and keep wishing for things I couldn't have.

Finally, I ignored it. I grabbed the blanket from the back of the couch, wrapped it around me, and settled in alone for a long winter's night.

31

CHRISTA

"Mmmmmm." I woke, stretched, sniffed…coffee?

My eyes opened to bright light, pouring in through the bedroom's single window. Not home. I blinked fully awake. The cabin in the woods. Micah's. The man who'd saved me and then…

Fueled by panic, I turned and put my arm out, only to pull it back in pain.

Oh, holy night, my *back*. It was worse than yesterday. I felt steamrollered, like every bone and muscle had been pried apart and hammered at before being put back into my body.

But worse than that, I was alone. And had been for a while, judging by the coolness of the sheet beside me. Not to mention the sweet smells coming from the kitchen. Had he even slept here with me or had he spent another night on the sofa?

I cocked my head, expecting to hear some kind of movement from the other room.

Nothing. Absolute silence.

Not only was there no sound, but there was no...presence.

Something big and heavy and sad weighted my chest. Which was ridiculous, right? He'd probably let the dogs out and no doubt had a million other things to take care of out there.

But his absence felt like more than that. It felt like a message, a *Don't get too comfortable, Christa. And definitely don't get too used to this.*

I let out a shaky breath, keeping it as measured and quiet as I could. No point feeling sorry for myself. Besides, it wasn't over yet.

At least I didn't think so.

I swallowed hard and glanced at the window. Okay, so it had stopped snowing, he was awake and gone and I was alone.

We'd have today, still, I guessed. And possibly tomorrow. Maybe longer, depending on snow plows and stuff like that. But this *thing* wouldn't last much longer. It couldn't.

But when it was over, I'd be devastated.

I would not freaking cry again. Especially not about the *amazing* sexual experience we'd shared. He'd rattled me. I'd rattled myself, if I was honest. But I refused to get melancholy before it even ended. Nope.

Faster than was good for me, I rolled to the side of the bed and sat up. *Whoa.* That hurt. I waited for the sharper pains to subside and wrapped the thick, down-filled comforter around me.

This pain wasn't all bad. Because today, I was sore for the right reasons, along with the wrong ones. Oh, I felt the accident, and probably would for months to come, but a new series of pains had emerged, sweet ones, where Micah had held me or stretched me, or where our bodies had rubbed each other raw. There was a luxuriousness to it. And a wistfulness that I—

Shut up.

I didn't have shoes or a purse or a phone or even conditioner for my hair. Right now, I would settle for clothes. Preferably clean ones. Or maybe something that smelled like him.

Idiot.

I stood and waddled to a dresser, wondering how rude it would be to open a drawer and rifle through it. Very, probably, but I couldn't exactly walk around the place in a feather-stuffed cape.

The first drawer contained neatly-folded boxer briefs. I closed it quickly…and then opened it again. Man, he was neat. His belongings all put away, the piles tidier than anything I'd created in my life.

The front door opened with the usual sound of eight tiny dog paws, and I slammed the drawer shut guiltily, and opened the bedroom door, still clad in nothing but a comforter.

"Hey!" I called out cheerily.

At the same time, he said, "You want to—"

Both dogs barked hysterically, overlapping our awkward moment. Things turned to chaos as they rushed back outside.

"Hold on. Something's out there." Micah gave me a quick look before following them outside.

I'm not sure why I hung back. Regular old caution, maybe, and the fact that I was buck-ass naked under the man's blanket. Whatever instinct it was, it sent me back into the bedroom to listen. Eventually, I heard the sound that had gotten them all so stirred up—an engine.

I should have been relieved. If someone was driving out there, then I had a chance of getting home today.

Hadn't I just fantasized about shoes and panties and flowery-smelling hair products? Wasn't I supposed to be happy at the prospect of Christmas with my Gran? Piles of food and presents and bittersweet holiday music? Shouldn't I want to get back to my life by now?

The answer was *yes* to all of the above. I should want every one of those things.

I didn't.

32

MICAH

*M*icah

Pete Carter's tractor made it about halfway up my drive before he gave up and hoofed it the rest of the way.

And because it was Pete and not that Jonathan Crandle King of the McMountain shithead, I went inside for the coat and boots I'd just taken off, ignoring the smell of coffee and fine woman I'd be leaving behind. Because Carter only ever came up here for real emergencies.

"Probably gonna need to take off, Christa. You be okay in there?"

"Oh. Oh, yeah. Sure."

"You got everything you need?"

"Course."

Carter knocked—polite, as always—before sticking his head in. "Got a crew down there needs you. Trees on the line and their truck's stuck." He made that funny little clicking sound in his mouth and turned, as if looking for a place to spit his chew. "Idiots."

"Be right there," I told him, ignoring his curious look as he went back out.

Once he'd gone a few steps, I turned to Christa. "Grab whatever clothes you need from the drawers. Feed the fire. There's breakfast. It'll probably be a while."

"Okay. Thank you."

I wanted to go in there and kiss her, warm my cold, rough outdoor hands on that soft, inviting skin of hers, but there wasn't time. Instead, I turned and stomped off through the snow, convinced I'd just missed out on something big.

Carter and I spent the next five hours getting a power company crew out of a jam. They shouldn't have been out here to begin with, but now that rich assholes had started buying up the mountain, the pressure must be on. People who had no idea how to survive without their fucking espresso machines and hot tubs.

They should be forced to stay home without cell service or wifi for a few days, maybe come to terms with the real person inside instead of posting fake-life selfies on fuckstagram.

And here I was aiding and abetting that behavior by helping out the power crews. Obviously, these guys weren't to blame. In fact, these were the ones who'd left their families on Christmas Day to help those jerks.

God, I hated society.

33

CHRISTA

*T*here was only so much napping and staring at the fire, petting the dogs, and reading tool catalogues that I could do before getting antsy. I'm a terrible cook and the last thing I wanted to do was ruin perfectly good ingredients by messing with them, so I drank coffee and snuggled with the girls and dozed. Overall, it was a pretty lovely way to spend Christmas morning.

Or it would have been, if Micah had been there.

So, when Bear barked, followed a few minutes later by the sound of footsteps tromping across the front porch, I was so excited I couldn't keep myself from running to the door. I threw it open and...

The smile melted off my face.

"What the fuck?" Jonathan Crandle, ex-boss, dickhead extraordinaire, and the last person I wanted to see right now, stared at me from under the hood of his fur-lined parka, open-mouthed, red-faced, and sweaty.

I fought the urge to step back and close the door, lock it, pretend I couldn't see or hear him, and go hide in Micah's bed. No way would I show this guy any sign of fear or weakness.

"How'd you end up here...Christa, honey?" Even out of breath, he managed to be repulsive. His eyes slid down my front, lingering on where my braless breasts strained the fabric of Micah's long-sleeved T-shirt.

Honey? Was he fucking kidding me? I folded my arms over my chest. "What did you call me?"

"Christa? That is your name, right?" He chuckled, though it sounded more like a gasp. Had he walked here? "Had a girl worked for me for two years before I realized she was Marian and not Marilyn. Or maybe the other way around." He shrugged, signifying how little that silly story of mistaken identity—or rather sheer idiocy—impacted him. It was all I could do not to kick him in the testicles. Again.

"What are you doing here, Jonathan?"

"Oh, funny story." Speaking overly loud, as usual, he put his hands out, palms forward like he always did when chatting with a new customer or starting a presentation. "Power went out. And... well, I've got the gas fire, but um, that's out too. And the generator's dead, so...I'm stuck without heat."

"Sorry to hear that."

"So…" He leaned in and looked over my shoulder into the cabin. The dogs growled from where they stood by my feet. "The man of the house around? Thought he might…"

"Might what?" Micah's voice, quiet and low, cut through the tension.

We both jumped. I'd gotten such tunnel vision from the anger this guy brought out in me that I hadn't heard him approach. He stood at the bottom of the porch steps, his face blank. He appeared calm and unthreatening.

I knew better.

"Oh, hey, neighbor!" Jonathan's fake friendly voice made me want to puke. "Hoped you might have some heat or shelter or…gas for a guy in need."

"No." Micah's steps took him up the stairs, forcing Jonathan to scoot to the side or be plowed through, and straight to my side. He wrapped an arm around me. "Next question."

"Uh. Question? Well, I'm not… I can't…" Jonathan blinked fast, his eyes darting between us. "You wouldn't let a man die out here on his own would you, neighbor?"

"I'd be tempted."

"Are you two—"

"None of your business." Wow. Implacable, hard Micah was sexy. In a scary kind of way. A muscle ticked in his cheek and the hand at my waist was tight and possessive.

"No, actually, you know what, Jonathan?" I put a placating hand on Micah's and stepped forward, hardly feeling the cold of the porch floor against my sock-clad feet. "It is a little bit your business, isn't it? Because you're the one who *forgot*." I used air quotes, because we all knew he hadn't forgotten a thing. "To tell me that the company holiday party was canceled. You're the one who plied me with booze before telling me that nobody else was actually coming. And you're the one who pulled out your penis and peed off your porch before putting your hands on my body against my will. Which, for the record, Jonathan, is *sexual battery* in this state."

"Oh, come on. You've got to be—"

Micah made a move and I stopped him with a straight arm, fueled by righteous anger. "I almost died because of you, Jonathan. I came out of your driveway on a night when nobody should have been driving on this mountain—which you knew since you canceled the damn party— swerved and went off the road." He opened his mouth, but no way was I letting him get a word in. "I hung there, stuck in my car on the side of a cliff for God only knows how long before Micah came and found me. He risked his life saving mine. So that's what I'm doing here, you disgusting excuse for a human being. I'm celebrating Christmas with a *real* man. The best man I've had the honor to meet. The kind of man who saves women instead of assaulting them."

Jonathan's round, disbelieving eyes flicked from Micah to me and back. "Come on now, you can't—"

"Goodbye." I turned and walked back inside, followed by the dogs and, after a few long seconds in which silent threatening messages were likely passed from one man to another, Micah. He closed the door firmly and locked it.

"I want to kill him."

I nodded, so full of adrenaline that just that small movement made me dizzy. "I know. I'm so thankful you didn't."

He went to the window and looked out before closing the curtains. "Fucker's not leaving."

"He won't." I wasn't sure how I knew this, but I did. "He's got no idea how to survive out here." Which meant he'd die if left to his own devices. And though I hated the man, watching him freeze to death on Micah's front porch wasn't something I could let happen.

"I'll give him our gas." *Our* gas. Wasn't it funny that he said it that way?

"And carry it up to his place for him?" He opened his mouth and I interrupted. "And how long will it last? Clearly, the guy's guzzling energy."

"Probably got his whole fucking house rigged up to the generator." Micah sighed. "Fuck."

I nodded. "So, we invite him in?"

34

MICAH

"I'll take him to town."

Christa's brows rose. "I thought you couldn't drive in this."

"Shouldn't. But Pete Carter plowed the road down to where the power crews worked today and the county plowed up to that level. We can get out in my truck."

I tried to suck in a deep breath and only filled my lungs about halfway. Why'd they hurt so much?

"So…you'd take him down and come back?" She didn't look any happier about it than I felt. Which was good, I guess.

I didn't mention that by the time we got down there, the roads would be refrozen and I couldn't drive back up. I moved to the fire, threw in a couple logs to safeguard my pipes from freezing, as much as possible.

"I can drop you at your place, too." I flashed a

smile her way. "You can be with your grandma for Christmas."

"Oh." She ran her hand over my desk, looking…sad, maybe? Couldn't be. She'd be going home. Should be ecstatic.

"We'll bring the dogs."

"Okay."

The asshole stomped across the porch and pounded at my door. Could I keep myself from pounding in his skull?

Ignoring him, I breathed deeply and eyed her bare feet. "You need shoes."

"What are you, like size 14?"

"We'll stuff 'em with socks."

At her nod, I went and packed a bag full of extra clothes, a sleeping bag, a couple blankets, just in case, and a bunch of dog food. She slipped into a pair of my boots and, though she claimed to look clownish and ridiculous, I'd never seen anything more adorable in my life.

Fuck, I had it bad.

"Hey, man!" Crandle pounded at the door again. "I'll pay you! Just let me in."

The only reply he got was the dogs barking.

With everything packed and Christa all bundled up, I sucked in a regretful breath and reached for the front door.

"Hey, guys, what's the—"

"Taking you to town."

"Oh, man. That's great. Great, thank you. You can drop me at—"

"The city limits. You can get a cab from there. Or a schmuber or whatever the fuck it is assholes like you get around in."

"Well, hey, that's a little—"

The pressure in my skull popped. I dropped my bag to the snow, turned, and grabbed him by the collar of his ridiculous bomber jacket. With my face real close to his, I whispered, "The only reason you're standing right now is 'cause Christa wouldn't let me beat your face in. As far as I'm concerned, you're nothing but a sub-human piece of excrement. If she'd let me, I'd break every bone in your body." I dropped him to the ground, but kept my hold for a few beats longer. "But *she* gets to choose because she's the one you hurt with your fuckhead actions. So, be glad you're alive and not just a puddle of meat and blood in the snow." I let him go, turned to the truck, and opened up the tailgate. "You're riding in back."

When he opened his mouth to argue, I threw him one of the blankets and opened the passenger door for Christa and the girls. We settled in and I inched the truck down the drive.

After a few minutes, Christa turned to me. "I don't even want to look."

"He'll be fine."

"I can't believe you made him ride in back."

"Asshole was lucky I parked in the barn. Otherwise, he'd be ass-deep in snow right now."

When she didn't respond, I glanced at her.

She turned quickly to look out the window, shoulders stiff.

Shit. Had I upset her? Did I do something wrong?

We rode down the mountain in silence, except for the occasional rattle of a collar when one of the girls shifted. Christa spent the entire trip looking out the window, her hand buried in first Brownie's fur and then Bear's. I wished she'd put it in my lap, instead. I wished she'd look my way.

The trip took twice as long as usual, even once we hit the bigger road. "He okay back there?"

She looked over her shoulder. "Alive."

"Hell. Maybe I should drive faster."

Her smile dropped the second the city limits appeared. Right beyond the sign was a grocery store and a chain motel. A perfect place to drop the asshole off. I pulled over, put the truck in park and walked around to open up the tailgate.

He slid to the ground and glared at me, muttered some shit about uneducated freaks, and stomped off.

I didn't care. Though if he'd insulted her, he'd be on his ass right now.

It took a few deep breaths and got back in the truck.

"Where to, Christa?"

35

CHRISTA

hrough the fogged-up window, I blinked at the passing houses and their bright Christmas lights, wishing I knew what to say to make this last.

Not much for relationships. His sentence kept going through my mind, the way it had all the way from the top of the mountain. And now that I knew him a little better, I could understand. The man had his ways, a life he'd set up exactly how he needed it. In order to survive, after the horrible things he'd lived through. While at *war*, for God's sake.

So, no I didn't understand. I couldn't possibly.

"Left here," I said, swallowing back the words I really wanted to say. *Turn back. I want to stay with you.*

He didn't do relationships.

But this didn't feel like that at all. *Relationship* was such a silly word. Relate. Relating to each other seemed like much too small a thing when this felt like…everything.

*Belonging*ship. *Knowing*ship. Ha!

I almost laughed. *Holy shit, the drama going on in my head right now.*

About one damned weekend.

Maybe I'd take something less than a relationship with him. Maybe I'd accept whatever he wanted to give me.

"It's up here, on the right. You can pull into the drive." *Since we don't have a car anymore.*

Oh, God. I pressed my fingers to my eyeballs. I'd deal with *that* later.

I took in a breath and watched Gran's house, wishing this didn't feel so wrong.

"Wanna come inside?"

"I'll walk you to the door."

I nodded, tightened my hand in Brownie's fur and then Bear's. I'd miss these two. Which was ridiculous, after less than two days. Then again, it was nothing compared to how much I'd miss him.

I opened the door and slid out, then started up the front walk, which had been shoveled. Hm. Interesting. Had she paid someone? On Christmas Day? That was impressive.

Slowly, and not just because of the massive shoes on my feet, I went up the steps and put my hand on the doorknob. He caught up to me and, for a few seconds, I just stared at him. *Kiss me. Stay with me. Don't go back home tonight. Take me with you.*

My chest hurt and my sinuses stung. Rather

than look at him another second—and risk letting it all pour out—I turned the knob, stepped inside and—

Froze for a good five seconds, barely comprehending what I was seeing. It wasn't until Micah's hand landed on my shoulder and tugged me back out that I snapped out of it and slammed the door shut.

"*Ohhhhhhhhhhhhh my God.*"

"Guess Granny's doing just fine without you." Was he laughing?

I forced my eyes back open. There wasn't a hint of humor on his face. "That was awful, Micah. I need to wash my brain."

From inside came the sound of scuffling. Gran and Gus struggling to get their clothes back on, no doubt. Holy shit. I needed a drink or something. Right now.

"Christa? Oh, God. I'm so sorry honey," she yelled loud enough to be heard through the door. When it didn't immediately open, I leaned in.

"Everybody okay in there?"

"Yep. Just grand." Gran laughed. "I can't open the door, though. I'm…I'm not ready to see that look on your face again."

Micah grabbed my hand and squeezed it. His face was bright red with suppressed laughter.

I squeezed him back and managed a smile. Okay. So, my grandmother was getting some. This wasn't a bad thing. I was only sorry that I'd had to see it. And that I'd almost lost my life to a heart attack.

I thumped my chest, wondering if I'd ever breathe normally again.

"Gonna open the door now."

"That's a good idea." I stepped back, assuming Micah would let go of my hand. He didn't.

Gran looked remarkably put together, considering the parts of her body that had been exposed just minutes before. Behind her, Gus, new neighbor and, apparently more than friend, stood looking stiff and formal. They were flushed, which I couldn't entirely assume was due to embarrassment, given how acrobatic their movements had been.

Oh, God. I closed my eyes and opened them again with a forced smile.

"I'm ah…sorry to bust in on you guys."

"No. Nope. Our fault." Gran backed into the room, opened the door wider to invite us in. "Let us never mention it again. Didn't happen."

"Good plan," Micah said.

"Are you Micah?" Gran's eyes looked from his face to mine, down to our joined hands and back up again.

"Yes, ma'am."

All the tension and strained humor in the atmosphere morphed in a flash when Gran stepped forward, wrapped her arms around Micah, and burst into tears.

Oh. *Oh.*

He stood awkwardly for a few seconds before hugging her back.

"Thank you for saving my grandbaby's life, Micah. For giving me the best Christmas gift I could ask for."

When she finally pulled away, Gus the neighbor, whose last name I didn't know, but who'd been intimate as hell with my grandma, shook Micah's hand.

"Thank you, son. Thank you."

Jesus. What a roller coaster.

"Come in," said Gran. "All the heat's leaving and—"

"Oh, I gotta—" Micah couldn't get more than a few words past my grandmother.

"No. No, you come in and have a drink or a cocoa or—"

"Dogs are in the truck. Better get going." He stepped back, stiff and stubborn. "Have a great one."

"You sure, son?" Gus narrowed his eyes at Micah.

"It's ah…been…" He turned to Gran. "Really nice meeting you, ma'am. Sir." He cleared his throat a couple times and glanced my way. "Christa."

I opened my mouth to say something, to ask him to stay, maybe, to tell him…something. But it didn't come fast enough. As I stood there, trying my damnedest to come up with something, he was gone.

He didn't want this. He didn't want me.

Taking off without a real goodbye proved it. He'd go back to his house, to his simple life and I'd go back to…

I shut my eyes against the painful prick of tears, and swallowed.

No strings. No relationships. He'd told me that. And I'd been okay with it, then. Before.

It didn't feel so good right now. It felt like a loss, and I'd had enough of those to recognize the sensation.

Then again, how could I lose something I'd never had?

36

MICAH

I knocked, which felt like a weird thing to do, since I'd grown up in this house.

Cindy yanked open the door, letting out a warm waft of Christmas that wrapped me like a blanket. Like home.

"Oh. My. Gawd. Mom! *Mooooom!*" Cindy screamed like she used to when we were kids, and took off at a run, leaving me standing in the doorway like a dick. "*It's Micah!*"

"What? What?" Mom sounded just as crazed. She hurried from the kitchen, nearly crashing into my sister, and stopped at the end of the hall, breathless.

After that, it was mayhem. Kids crawled out of the woodwork. There was Christmas shit everywhere—streamers and lights, people in ridiculous sweaters bumping into each other to get to me.

Everybody piled on top of me with hugs and

kisses and questions. My brothers-in-law, dudes I barely knew, patted me on the back. Someone shoved a cold beer into my hand. I pressed it to my forehead.

A screechy carol blasted in the living room. Somebody'd better turn it down before I—

Brownie bumped my leg and I reached for her. Bear ate up the attention from my nieces and nephews, but Brownie'd never been one for crowds. I dug my fingers into her fur and rubbed, not sure who I was trying to calm.

"D'you get the gifts? Amber made the…"

"Did someone save a piece of cake? Micah needs cake. There's…"

"Hey! Turn off the…"

"Damn, bro, you're hairier every time I…"

They accepted my presence, like they'd known I'd make it back, eventually. Like a hug I'd never asked for.

I fought to breathe through all the heat and chaos.

Shit. I couldn't take this noise. All the noise, noise, noise, noise, *noise!*

I pressed my fists into my eyeballs and jolted when a hand tightened on my arm.

"Come here." Dad tilted his head toward the back of the house and led the way, hair grey, shoulders stooped, walking slow. Jesus, when did I last see him? A couple months ago? I racked my brain until it came back. Drew's birthday. Spring. Had I really avoided my family since then?

Probably.

He led me into his office, which was off-limits to the kids.

"Sit down." Dad liked playing the big man, ordering me around. I didn't mind. It was his place, his family. He was a good father. Wanted us happy.

I sat in his big, beat-up armchair and watched him pour scotch into a couple glasses. He handed me one and clinked his against it before settling into the chair opposite mine.

Brownie's tail thumped on the carpet when Dad bent to give her a quick rub.

"What brings you here today, son?"

I opened my mouth to say something about Christmas, but it wasn't the answer I needed to give.

"Met a woman."

He nodded slowly, sipping his drink and looking like he knew shit I'd never understand.

"Where is she?"

"At her grandmother's."

"And you're here."

I opened my mouth and shut it. Took a big swig of the smoky booze, enjoyed the burn in my belly. "I freaked out. Left."

"That good, huh?" His smirk was all-knowing.

"Her?" I couldn't help but grin in return. "She's amazing."

"Why aren't you with her, then?"

"Only met her a couple days ago." That didn't seem right. *Was* that right? Christ, it sounded like a lie after what we'd had or done or shared. I'd known her for centuries. A lifetime.

His brows rose. "You giving her space or something?"

"Hell if I know." Another slow sip, letting the booze warm me. I bent forward. "That story you always tell about you and Mom. How you knew the night you met her. Is that true?"

Dad leaned back in his chair and grinned up at the ceiling. "Yeah. Had a girlfriend at the time, too."

"No shit."

He nodded once. "Jeanette or Jean or something. Didn't matter. Met your mother. The real deal. Called the girlfriend the next morning to break it off. Felt like cheating just knowing that your mom existed." He leveled me with his hard, bad-ass dad stare. "What's this woman's name?"

"Christa. Evans. She's um…" Jesus, now I had to find words to describe the woman who'd felled me in two days? I exhaled, long and low. "Guess she… Well, she looks like the woman in those Australian murder mysteries mom loves so much."

"Ha!" Dad shouted out a laugh. "Miss Fisher?"

"Yeah. Kinda acts like her, too. Not embarrassed to be…herself." I couldn't help a smile, though my chest hurt. "Jesus. We just walked in on her grandmother making out with an old guy."

Dad barked out a laugh. "And you left her alone with them? What's wrong with you, boy?"

Shit. I had, hadn't I? I stood, slugged the drink back and set it on Dad's desk.

"You're right. Better go."

"Sneak out the back. I'll explain to your mother." Dad rose slowly and put his hand on my shoulder. When had my hands gotten bigger than his? "Don't wait nine months before coming next time. And bring Christa."

Maybe I'd do that.

37

CHRISTA

*S*omeone pounded at the door and I almost dropped the plate I was drying. I put it down, carefully. It was him. Had to be. Who else could it be?

And, because I had absolutely no pride when it came to Micah Graham, I ran to the door and threw it open. "You're ba—"

I was dangling from his arms before I could finish the sentence, his lips hot on mine. He devoured me like he'd never get another chance. Like this was it.

And this *was* it. It *was*.

He eventually pulled away, probably to breathe or something, and let me slide to my feet, keeping me warm in his embrace.

"Couldn't stay away." The words were hot puffs on my mouth. "Don't want to."

"I don't want you to, either, Micah."

"Good. Good." He nodded, and I noticed

how cold the tip of his nose was against my cheek.

"Come inside." I turned, paused and looked at him over my shoulder. "Stay the night."

"Oh, no. Your gran's place. I'm not—"

"What? What? Oh, don't mind us," Gran called, emerging from the hall in a rush. "We'll give you some privacy."

I flushed red as a beet at the sly expression on her face. It took a few seconds to realize that she and Gus were quickly suiting up to go outside. As if they'd been waiting for an excuse to be on their own again.

"Oh, you don't have to—"

"We're leaving you the house." She wrapped a scarf around her mouth. "End of discussion." The words came out muffled, but final.

"Okay, Gran."

"And your dogs are welcome to stay, too, Micah. Too cold for them out there."

"Thank you, ma'am."

"Alice," she corrected before wishing us a happy Christmas, with an extra-long hug for both of us. Micah and I watched them disappear into the cozy, streetlamp-lit snow scene.

The door shut and, while the dogs performed a thorough investigation of the house, Micah and I stood by the door. It was awkward in the silence of this house that wasn't even mine, with this man who'd come back for me, this man I'd only just met, but who felt like he'd somehow looked into my soul.

I turned toward the kitchen. "Can I get you a drink or—"

"No." He stepped forward, cradled my face in his hands, and leaned down. "I want to go to bed with you. Now. I want to sleep and wake up and hold you in the morning."

The kiss he gave me felt like so much more than just a touch. He was pouring emotion into me, telling me things he had a hard time communicating in words.

"I want that."

"For longer than tonight." He glanced at the door. "Tomorrow. And the next day."

"I thought you didn't do relationships." The last word came out breathless, as inconsequential as air.

"Thought so, too."

"What changed your mind?"

"*You.*" He rubbed his nose to mine, gently, slowly. "Us."

"We barely know each other." Strangely, this didn't feel true, but I had to say it.

"I know you." A long, slow slide of his rough cheek against mine. "I *know* you, Christa Evans."

"How'd this happen?" I whispered.

Was I obsessed because he'd saved my life? Possibly. *Maybe?* How could I not be? And while it wasn't necessarily the best idea to start a relationship like this, *so what?*

Lifelong friendships could be built on a person saving another's life, right? I'd heard stories about that. Couldn't love happen the same way? Would it somehow be more kosher if we'd met at a dinner party or a bar?

Hell, no.

"Don't know how it happened and I'm not gonna question it. I don't want to be the loner on the mountain anymore, avoiding life. The people I love. Besides…" he leaned in close "…couldn't leave you with two seventy-year-olds making out like teenagers on the sofa."

I shuddered with a grin. "Don't remind me."

"Guy must have moves, though, getting it on with the hot granny on Christmas Day."

"I *guess*."

"I want that when I'm eighty. And I'm a lucky bastard." He kissed me again, slow and wet and deep. By the end, he had to hold me up. "'Cause I already found the woman to do it with, Christa Evans, and I'm never letting her go."

EPILOGUE

One month later...

"We'll be late, Micah."

"Just give me another minute." I tightened my arm around the warm, pliant body in my arms, put my nose to Christa's nape and inhaled her the way I consumed food or air. Like I needed it to survive. I had to get her taste in my mouth.

I tore the comforter back. Giggling, she put her hand on mine to stop me. "No time."

"It'll be quick," I promised, anchoring her hip with one palm while I shimmied down, muttering that I just needed enough to tide me over for the rest of the day.

"This is important, Micah, you're gonna make me look..."

I shouldered her thighs apart, sucked in a

deep, happy breath, and took a long, slow look before pulling her lips open and licking her good morning.

"*Ooooooooooooh, God.*"

This. This was the stuff, right here—endless spooning, slow, half-asleep kisses, easy, honest conversations, languid sex with our eyes still shut, and my girlfriend's pussy in the morning, wet and waiting. Wanting me the way I wanted her—with this constant, aching hunger—except a good hunger. The kind worked up from a long, hard day's work.

I licked her hot, sweet place, ran my nose along the plush softness, nibbled for about five seconds and finally let myself taste inside.

A swipe of my tongue up and up until I reached her little jewel of a clit. Time was of the essence, so I took it between my lips and sucked before flicking it with my tongue in the way that made her lose her mind.

Almost immediately, Christa's body shook with those quick, urgent pants that told me her climax was seconds away. Except we didn't have time for multiple orgasms this morning. We had time for one. And I wanted hers to happen on my cock.

"Hold on, baby," I whispered, climbing her body until I was lined up with her and, though I'd planned to slide right in, I stopped, frozen in place.

In the space of a few seconds, her expression

morphed from that lost, heavy-eyed, wet-lipped look to worry.

"Micah?" Her gaze searched mine. "What is it?"

Unable to talk through the tightness in my chest, I shook my head.

"Baby?" Her hand stroked my cheek. "Tell me?"

"I love you." Well, shit. There. It was out.

She opened her mouth and shut it again, did that a couple more times and then, as if she'd lost the power of speech, grasped my head between both hands and lifted her mouth to kiss me. Hard, like an owning. *Mine*, she said, with her lips and teeth and tongue. Like, for once she was the one at a loss for words.

My response was just as wild. And that was one more thing that made sense between us. Though we could be sweet as hell, we lost it in each other's arms.

And this kiss was absolutely feral. A mauling. I'd be surprised if we didn't draw blood. And somehow, suddenly, the head of my dick was right at her entrance and I was partway in.

I took penetration slowly with her, usually, but telling her I loved her had somehow made me savage. I thrust hard enough to shove us up against the headboard.

"I love you," I gasped again as she tightened around me. "I love you so fucking bad, Christa."

"Yeah," she gasped. I thrust again and she

moaned, drawing a growl from the depths of my soul. My hips worked back and forward, claiming her with a mind of their own.

"I love your pussy. I want to own it. Want it tight around me every day. Every morning. Every night, I want to pound you like this." My voice sounded like shit. Low and animal and mean.

"Oh, crap, Micah. Oh, God."

I leaned to the side, put my weight on one arm, and pinned her to the bed with my other hand on her belly, then slowly withdrew. "Fuck, baby, I'll never get tired of seeing those pussy lips around my cock. Look at how you're stretched tight, all glossy and juicy for me. Taking me in." I thrust hard, drawing a low, ugly sound from her —the kind of sound I lived for. "Take it, Christa." Another hard thrust. "Take my love. Take my cock."

"I want it," she whispered, the words more breaths than actual sounds. "I want you."

"Yeah. Fuck, yeah. Take me." My cock, shiny and steel-stiff plowed back inside and, fuck I wanted to watch some more—for hours—but from the glassy look in her eyes, she was about to come and I had to go with her.

"You there, sweetheart? Huh? You almost there?"

She tightened her fingers on my ass, pulled me in deep, grunted a response, and, goddamn, I loved how my woman lost her words with me.

"All right, I'm gonna do it." I swallowed,

trying to remember how to say the things I needed to express—dirty talk always made her hotter, made her orgasms flame brighter. "I'm gonna pound this little pussy until you come all over my cock. And then I'm gonna fill you up."

My voice broke, along with my mind. "Fuck. Fuck. I fucking love you. Love your pussy. Love *you*."

My last few thrusts were mindless and messy, probably too strong, but I was gone, lost in her, coming harder than I had in my life and—*Fuck. Fuck me, this. This. This was it.*

In the seconds before we lost it together, she watched me, her gaze so full that tears rushed my eyes.

This.

With a roar of relief, I let go just as her pussy clamped around me. Everything blurred.

I wanted to pull her in tight, to hide from the intensity, but I couldn't, because she was it and I wanted her to see that.

This.

I was too heavy for her, though she always claimed to like this moment when I truly let go and gave her everything. My heart was still thwacking against the inside of my ribcage when my vision finally cleared and my brain told me take some of this weigh off her or she'd suffocate. I straightened my arms.

"Love you, too, Micah." Her pussy tightened around me and she put a hand to the side of my face, where she caught a tear with her fingers. Huh. I was crying. "This is it for me, too." Had I said that aloud a few minutes ago? "You, Micah. You're it for me."

She smiled and I'd just started to move inside her again when the alarm blasted through the moment.

"Shit," I muttered as she shoved at me.

Now we were definitely gonna be late.

Micah opened my door and grabbed my hand as I slid from his truck, then pulled the seat forward to let the girls out. I hung back and looked at the house.

It was average-looking. Built in the 80s, I guessed. White siding with black shutters. Pretty big—unsurprising, given how many kids they'd had. The lawn was partially hidden under a crusted layer of snow, but it looked well-tended.

"You okay?" Micah eyed me in that way that made me feel like he saw beneath my outer layers, into the real soft core of me. "Can hardly tell with that big-ass coat on."

"Well whose fault is that, then?" I forced humor into my voice, even though I was frankly scared. He'd insisted I get something warm for up there at his place. And, yeah, he'd been right, but I looked like a freaking dumpling in this thing.

"It's cute on you."

"Cute. Great. Here I was going for sophisticated and serious for your—"

"Oh my God, he's here!" A woman yelled from the porch. "You guys! They're—"

Seconds later, she was joined by another woman—Cindy, maybe—then a couple kids.

"Micah! Micah, look at my new princess shoes. They're—"

"Bear! Here, boy!"

"It's a girl, dummy. Don't you—"

Voices overlapped, the dogs joining in, and within seconds what felt like about twelve families spilled out onto the snow-covered front lawn.

"Micah's here! With his giiiiirlfriend! She's so—"

"Get back in, Tony, you're barefoot! You'll catch—"

A toddler rushed out between two adults, stumbled down the steps and made a beeline for them. In two long strides, Micah got to her and scooped her up. He put his bearded face to her belly and had her giggling in half a second. I slowed, my eyes taking in this new version of the man I loved.

Love.

The word hit me in the belly, made my steps falter and my heartbeat go wild. I wondered, for a second, how I could contain this much emotion for the man. After a second's hesitation I caught up to him, wide-eyed and out of breath.

His eagle eyes had witnessed my off-kilter

moment. He leaned in, and put his forehead to mine. "Want to get out of here?" he whispered.

Yes. This was a lot for an only child, even if I was pretty comfortable with people. This wasn't a crowd. It was a mob. A horde. "Course not."

He gave me a quick peck on the lips and stood up straight again. "Hey, everyone," he called. "This is Christa."

I smiled and waved, awkward as I headed up the walkway right into the heart of the throng. But as I walked, I realized, it was an overwhelming number of people and, yeah, they were incredibly loud, but they looked so *happy* to see us, so eager to meet me, that I couldn't help but feel welcomed.

"Christa!" A tall, thickly-built woman whose long face was capped with short, grey hair pushed her way through to the front of the crowd, hands outstretched. "Come on in, honey. Let's find you a quiet place so you can acclimate to..." She spread her arms with a grin. "Us."

Hours later, after lunch and birthday cake, gifts and games, Micah checked with me before disappearing down a hall with his dad—a big, softie of a man I immediately felt at home with. I turned to see his mom coming toward me carrying a couple mugs.

"Here. Herb tea." She handed me a cup and sank onto the sofa beside me, leaned in and said under her breath, "Or what I call a hot toddy." Her chin lifted to take in the room, which had finally almost emptied of people. "I imagine you'll need it after the Graham family hullaballoo."

"Thanks, Mrs. Grah—"

"Oh, honey." She sent an arch look my way. "I told you to call me Janie."

"Right." I smiled. "Thank you, Janie."

Cinnamon and clove steam rose from the mug, bringing me immediately back to the holidays and that first weekend with Micah.

"You're welcome." She took a sip and hummed happily, slipped off her shoes and drew her feet up under her. After a few seconds' silence, she sighed and turned to me. "Thank *you*, Christa."

"Oh. For the flowers? Well, of course—"

"No, honey. Not for the flowers. Or the gift for Payton, or for the casserole—which was delicious, by the way. Would your gran be willing to share the—" She clamped her mouth shut and shook her head with a self-deprecating look. "Thank you. For my son." She faced me full on now. When I didn't respond, she continued. "You don't get it, do you? You've given me the best present I could ever wish for. My baby went to war and he survived, thank goodness, but he never came back to us. We've glimpsed him maybe once a year for the past few years. Then, you fall into his life and suddenly, he's here all the time. You've brought my son back."

Overwhelmed by this outpouring of honest

emotion, I gulped from my drink, eyes stinging from the booze and the heat and, okay, yeah, from the tears, too.

"You don't have to say anything Christa, honey." Janie's hand grasped mine. "Just know that whatever's happening here, we approve." I opened my mouth, though I had no idea how to respond, but she just shook her head at me, sniffed, and squeezed my hand one last time before getting up to head back toward the kitchen.

Movement drew my eye to the other doorway and I knew, without a second's doubt, that it was him.

My man.

Everything else faded as our eyes met.

This thing between us—this *love*—felt new and raw as a fresh cut, fragile as a young sapling.

Delicate, but not weak, because for a new tree to survive in the forest, it would have to plant its roots deep, wouldn't it? There'd be work happening underground. It had to be strong to make it at all. Growth that our eyes couldn't see but that we'd feel. Like the work we'd done in our hearts.

Like this connection between us. This thing, the strongest emotion I'd ever felt, was as real to me as anything in my life. More real, maybe, since I could lose a car—the most expensive item I'd ever owned—and though it had been a heavy hunk of metal, it had no substance. It didn't matter like this did.

I'd come out of the that night with more than I'd had when I went in. I'd come out with everything.

"Ready?" I asked, full of warmth and spices and the love of this good man.

"Always," he said, without a trace of a smile. "*Always.*"

THE END

Christa and Micah have a bonus epilogue!
subscribepage.com/MountainManBonus

Get alerts when Adriana's books go live:
subscribepage.com/Releases

ACKNOWLEDGMENTS

I couldn't write a thing without my tribe—the inspiring and uplifting people I've been lucky enough to meet along the road to publication. I want to thank Amanda Bouchet, Kasey Lane, Alleyne Dickens, and Andie J. Christopher for reading early versions of this book. Thanks to Le Husband for being the best Happily Ever After a girl could wish for (and, yeah, I fell in love the night I met him!) and thanks to my readers for keeping me going. You guys are the best.

ALSO BY ADRIANA ANDERS

The Love at Last Series

Loving the Secret Billionaire

Loving the Wounded Warrior

The Survival Instincts Series

Deep Blue

Whiteout

The Blank Canvas Series

Under Her Skin

By Her Touch

In His Hands

ABOUT ADRIANA ANDERS

Adriana Anders is the award-winning author of the Blank Canvas and Love at Last series. Under Her Skin, a Publishers Weekly Best Book of 2017, has been featured in Bustle, USA Today Happy Ever After, and Book Riot and Loving the Secret Billionaire was a Romance Writers of America 2019 Rita® Award Finalist. Today, she resides with her tall French husband and two small children on the coast of France, where she writes the gritty, emotional love stories of her heart. Visit Adriana's Website for her current booklist: https://www.adrianaanders.com/

Made in the USA
Las Vegas, NV
13 February 2022

43844143R00139